SAVING SPADE

With great respect to Ian Jones.
Screenwriter of the film
The Lighthorsemen
and author of
A Thousand Miles of Battles

SAVING SPADE

DENNIS OGDEN

ISBN: 978-0-6480869-0-1   Softcover
        978-0-6480869-1-8   Ebook

Hame Cam Our Gudeman at E'en
from The Scotish Minstrel (1823)

The Dying Stockman By Banjo Paterson

The Overlanders published in the
Queensland Camp Fire Song Book in 1865.

Author bio and more:
www.ogdenimprint.com

CHAPTERS

Chapter 1
THE SOLDIER

February 1919
Fifty miles east of Kantara, Egypt

[Lewis]

Private Lewis Dunbar of the Australian 2nd Light Horse Brigade should be over the moon with relief and elation. The war said to end all wars is finally over. For the past two years he has fiercely and fearlessly fought battles across the harsh, arid Arabian deserts from Palestine to the Sinai Peninsula. In a matter of days, he'll be on a boat back home to Australia. Yes, he should be relieved and elated, but he's not. In fact, he's bloody well broken-heartedly crushed.

For some days now rumours have been spreading. Rumours that gnaw at the guts of every mounted soldier—their horses will be staying.

They could bring back diseases, they say. It would cost too much, they say. They! Who are they? No one who's planted their rear in a saddle, that's for sure. Or brushed down a horse and been nudged in the back by a playful friend. And obviously, nobody who's been on a trusted, courageous Waler as they charge into the gun sights of the enemy.

It's said, in the army, your best friend is your rifle. Maybe so, but in the Australian and New Zealand Light

Horse, it's just as much your faithful Waler. Now, with the war over, in Lewis Dunbar's mind, it's your horse that should never leave your side.

And what does '*stay here*' mean? Here in Egypt where the treatment of animals is harsh, or worse, they're butchered for food. Lewis will never abandon his horse Spade to end up on someone's plate or spend his days pulling a plough. Not after all they've been through. Now, the word is, they're ordering any horse over twelve years of age shot and skinned for leather.

It was about twelve years ago on Dunbar cattle station in the rugged Queensland north interior that Spade was born into Lewis' arms. A feisty, pure-blood Arabian colt. Chestnut in colour with a white diamond between his eyes that dribbled down to the tip of his nose.

Lewis was only a young fella then. Half Aboriginal from his mother's side. Half Scottish from his stout, ginger-haired, pale and freckled father, Magnus Dunbar.

Dunbar took over the pastoral lease of Yirandall station when he arrived in Australia. It was then running sheep, and being a sheep farmer back in Scotland, he soon realised why the previous leaseholder wanted out. Apart from the harsh dry land, the price of wool had plummeted. The sheep started getting liver fluke that reduced lambing. Those lambs that were born, were continually set upon by wild dingoes. And, on top of all that, the remoteness. It was more than obvious to Dunbar that the land was better suited for raising cattle. This was well before any thought of raising a son.

Maisie Dunbar was a slave to the previous station owner. When Magnus took over the place, he kept her on as his live-in housekeeper. She was then called by her Aboriginal name, Jippa Nampijinpa. She was loyal, cooked to her master's liking and kept the homestead clean and clear of Dunbar's worst fear—snakes.

Magnus was always exhausted after a long day overseeing the workings of the station. The logistics of changing the livestock to cattle was also challenging. So, after a hearty meal, he looked forward to a relaxing glass of whisky—Scotch, of course. A single malt whisky from the still of James Stewart & Co. Cases which he had specially imported from the Scottish Highlands by John M. Headrick & Co spirit merchants.

One night, after one too many glasses, he invited Jippa to keep him company. Jippa could not understand his tipsy chatter but liked the melody of his Scottish accent. These nights soon became regular and intimate, resulting in Jippa becoming pregnant. They married. After which Magnus changed Jippa's name to Maisie in memory of his mother who died back in Scotland.

At the birth of Lewis, the first thing that appeared was the top of his head tinged with ginger hair. The sight of this Scottish trait thrilled Magnus. He always assumed his Scottish genes to be far stronger than those of an Aboriginal. So it came as a shock when the expected fair-skinned baby boy emerged black. From that moment on the deflated Magnus had little to do with baby Lewis.

Maisie was left to care for and bring up her boy alone. She moved out of the homestead and in with the other Aboriginal workers—her own mob. Here, she taught Lewis their ways and his culture.

As Lewis grew older, leaner and taller, there was

always the stigma hovering over him that he was the boss's son. His Aboriginal facial features, while still dark, revealed a hint of the Scottish influence of his father. This slight resemblance was enough to be a constant reminder to all of where his heritage lay. At every chance, the station hands and drovers would tease him and always test his worth and his horsemanship. In the end, they were to change their opinion.

Everyone, including every horse, had to work for their tucker on the outback station. Even Lewis' adopted responsibility—the new-born foal. As a further test, Lewis, alone, had to raise and prepare the horse to drive the growing herd of cattle. First, was to wean him off mother's milk. Then, when he became stronger, Lewis would take him into the arid outback for extended periods. They'd sleep together under the stars and eat only what they found. Spade developed a fondness for a spinifex-like desert plant called Horse Mulla Mulla. Though the plant was edible, he much preferred their moist roots and would dig them up with his hoof. This action offered up the name Lewis had been searching for.

After years of training and maturing, Spade was ready. The pair joined the experienced drovers on longer and longer cattle drives. Within a month or two, Spade showed he could outsmart any cow, bull or heifer. On to them in a flash he was. Turned on a penny and side-stepped like a dancer. This skilful connection between horse and rider carried through to local rodeos. They performed tricks to the delight of the audience, young and old. One trick, in particular, stole the show. As Spade cantered around the arena, Lewis slid from his back, under his belly and between his striding front legs. As a finale, he'd pull himself up with arms around his horse's neck and kiss Spade on the nose. Their horse and rider skills had reached the highest peak.

When war broke out in 1914, Lewis had just turned sixteen. Though too young to enlist, he already knew the Light Horse was his destiny. It started when one of the drovers returned from the nearest town with a recruitment poster. Initially, it was of no interest to Lewis. News of the war had not reached his ears. Recruitment posters showed only a 'coo-ee' calling soldier straddling the Dardanelles with not a horse in sight. The drovers were eager to join up and that's when the Light Horse was all they talked about. The need for both man and horse convinced Lewis this was for him.

On turning eighteen, Lewis was old enough to enlist but had to be nineteen before being sent overseas. Waiting a year was not an option, and he lied that he was a year older. Of course, they had doubts about his age, but the need for more recruits had become crucial. The war was spreading over increasing fronts in Europe, Africa and the Middle East.

Despite the urgent need for recruits, Lewis still had to prove his ability in the saddle and on bareback. A test course consisted of a variety of jumps over logs, water and walls. He scaled all with ease. His knowledge of horses was hard to beat, and he passed his medical fitness test. Once done, they had no choice but to assign him for overseas duty.

There was also an urgent need for more strong 'Walers'. So called because, in Australia, it was wrongly assumed all stock horses of Arab breeding came from the state of New South Wales. As both Lewis and his horse impressed, the government purchased Spade for thirty pounds. They branded him with the British Commonwealth arrow on the rear left rump and an army number on one hoof. A rushed period of training for combat together with the use of firearms followed. Before he knew it, Lewis, Spade and hundreds of other horse and riders were on their way to Egypt to defend the Suez Canal. Places as unknown to them as the oceans they were about to cross.

For over two years Lewis and Spade saw action against the Ottoman Empire across the Sinai/Palestine frontier. Romani, Magdhaba, Rafa, Gaza, Jaffa, Es Salt and Beersheba were bloody battles that tested both man and beast. Many did not survive.

Now, the sun is setting on the war and the day. The remains of their regiment have set up camp at a small dried up wadi a day's ride away from Kantara on the eastern side of the Suez Canal. Once they get there, they'll decamp and wait for the vessel that will take the men—only the men—back home to Australia.

Lewis looks on as Spade lowers his head to drink from the makeshift canvas water trough. Down the length of the picket line other brave and battered Walers rest their weary bodies. Some are eating out of their nose bags. Some wear fly veils and flick their tails to deflect the annoying pests. All have served their country with valour.

He runs a hand over his horse's lean, taut and war-weary body. There's a slight twitch in Spade's foreleg. So many scars from desert nettles and the more severe scars from bullets, bayonets and shrapnel. Lewis relives each incident and how many times they faced death. Still, they made it through. But for what?

If them fellas don't let me take you back with me. It better I shoot you myself!

In a flash, Spade's head rears up from the trough. With eyes wide and white he snorts and backs away.

Did you hear what me tinkin'?

Lewis immediately throws his arms around his companion's neck and whispers in his ear. "Never, Spade…bloody never".

Spade nestles his head over Lewis' shoulder. They stay like this for ages. A bond that cannot…no, should not…no, damn it…*will* not be broken. As the day's light begins to follow the sun over the horizon, they remain in a mental conference. Lewis feels a determined nod of his horse's head on his shoulder. He slides his arms from around his neck and steps back. They look deep into each other's eyes. Spade gives another nod and a snort confirming the only acceptable solution.

"Drink up Spade. Tonight we ride long way."

Chapter 2
THE BEDOUIN GIRL

[A'isha]

A thick mist of fear and isolation is smothering me. Why am I being held captive by men in uniform? Some with hats that have a strange plume flowing from it. The odour they emit is hard to stomach. They mouth words I do not understand. Hands that have touched me are, I'm sure, the same hands that inflicted my injuries. I'm a Bedouin girl and by the laws of the desert not to be harmed…even in battle.

This tent I am in is small, hot and ill-erected. There is no camel hair woven carpet to cover the ground. No scattered colourful cushions. In fact, there is no colour at all. The canvas walls are grey, as is the uncomfortable bed I lie on. Am I to die here and never to see my family again? Never to marry and have my own family? My own tent?

The injury to my head throbs with the sound of a thousand racing camels. A crude bandage has replaced my head covering. My arm rests in a cloth tied around my neck. I can move my fingers without too much pain, so no bone is broken. My legs are undamaged so I can run. That, I must.

Born at the birth of the century, A'isha bin Saeed al Suhail is a slender, olive-skinned Bedouin girl. Her piercing dark brown eyes are windows to her dogged free will and inner strength. She has no memory of how she became captive. She is aware of the war and that her clan sided with neither the Turks nor the Westerners. They prayed only that the war would end, all those fighting would leave. Life would then carry on as it has since time began. Her peaceful tribe of Bedouin goat herders had only one aim in life—to seek pastures wherever and whenever to feed their flock. Now, with no other Bedouin in sight, she frets for her family.

Have my captors slain them all? Am I the only survivor? I cannot allow myself to believe such a thing. I must flee these evil men and find my family even if it means my death in the desert. Death in my chosen environment, harsh as it may be, would have the blessing of Allah.

A'isha runs her free hand over her drab olive green thobe and under her frayed brown headscarf now hanging over her shoulders. Her fingers feel along the woven camel hair braid tied around her neck. Three small goatskin parcels hang from the braid. Each is sealed with stitching of thin strips of leather. She clasps her hand around the first one to feel the loose dried cloves within. *Their scent and healing powers will comfort me.* In the third parcel, she feels the hard alum crystal within. *This will protect me against the 'evil eye'.* The middle leather pouch is larger. She feels its weight and strokes it, knowing that inside is a small scarab carved from green soapstone. *This scarab will ensure a renewal of life if I should forgo the one I now have.* Knowing all three parcels are intact reassures her that the talisman will protect her from Hasset and other evil Djinn spirits of the desert.

It is now time to plan my escape.

The flap of the small tent is suddenly pulled aside, allowing what cooling breeze there is to enter. For a moment a young medic blocks out the light as he enters. He is tall, lanky and stoops to fit into the tent erected to isolate the girl out of respect for her Bedouin custom. His long neck and protruding Adam's apple reminds A'isha of a desert vulture. He approaches leaving what lay beyond the tent open to view. From where she lies on her stretcher bed she sees tethered horses. Beyond them the beckoning, heat-shimmering desert and her freedom.

She attempts to raise herself up for a closer look, but a firm hand on her shoulder pushes her back down. Words, foreign to her, come from the young soldier. She looks into the eyes of her enemy as he speaks. *He'll never get a reply from me…never. For he does not know my voice failed to follow me at birth.*

He shakes his head at her silence. *Even if I had my voice, I would have cut out my tongue before uttering a word to him.* He removes the bandage on her forehead and checks the cut and bruising. The wound is cleaned and a fresh bandage applied. He raises each of her eyelids to examine her dark brown pupils. She would usually offer some resistance to his probing, but not this time. Instead, she fixes her eyes on his with a feral stare that would send wild dogs scampering. Her clenched lips force a fiery breath through her flaring nostrils. But all her facial posturing falls well short of its intended purpose. He readjusts the bandage on her arm and wiggles the protruding fingers. Content with the progress of her recovery, he places her arm back in the sling and gives her a nod and a smile. She ignores his attempt at being friendly. Accepting her healing has improved more than her attitude, the young medic leaves her side. She watches as he exits the tent, re-ties the flap straps, then speaks to the soldier standing guard outside.

If I am to be shot fleeing it will be as decreed by my fate, laid down before my birth as was my lack of voice. I will accept whatever befalls me, but I will not die here in this tent or anywhere else in the company of such enemies.

Chapter 3
THE ESCAPE

[Lewis]

With only a day or two to go before arriving at the main Kantara camp, rations are low. Long gone is a half decent meal of bully beef rissoles. The cooks now scavenge for whatever ingredients they can. Snakes, insects, some herbs and plants, the odd desert animal or wild dog, and if lucky, dates. Also, destined for the cooking pot was any horse not responding to treatment for a serious injury. Something the troopers had to put out of their mind and just swallow.

Lewis, with tin plate and mug in hand, is first in line at the makeshift field kitchen for the evening meal. There's no point in trying to hide his eagerness for food as everyone is hungry. His intention is not to satisfy his immediate hunger, but to rustle up enough of whatever is on offer to last at least two days. All that remains of his emergency rations is one hard tack biscuit. Hardly enough.

Slopped onto his tin plate is a watery gravy passed off as a stew of questionable ingredients. Not at all what he wanted. He was after something that was at least transportable. The stew would keep him going for a little while, so he ate it on the spot. The stale bread meant to soak up the gravy now accompanies the biscuit into his haversack. Little else was on offer so what he had would have to last. For how long? Like everything else, he had no idea.

Lewis waits anxiously for the sun to hide below the horizon. He's done all he can to ready Spade. Anything more in daylight would attract attention. When darkness finally comes, he places his haversack, a full water bottle and a half full grain sack under the saddle where it rests on the ground in front of Spade. His greatcoat, saddle wallets, heel rope, ground sheet roll and rifle bucket—considered unnecessary weight—lay in a pile under the saddle rug. The horseshoe case is all that's left attached to the saddle. Spade, like all the other horses, still wears his bridle. A head rope, strung through a ring of the jowl piece, is tied to the picket line. Lewis changes the knot to what he calls 'dem bloody robbers knot'. A quick release hitch knot that requires only one pull of the rope.

As the night hours pass the camp becomes relatively quiet. Lewis lies on his stretcher bed waiting for the snoring of his fellow tent-mates to be loud and steady. Confident all are sound asleep, he readies himself, dons his slouch hat and tugs it down securely. His trusted Lee-Enfield rifle lying beside him receives a mournful farewell stroke. Then, on hands and knees, he crawls to the tent opening. A glance back to make sure no one has stirred then pauses. They're his mates. Mates, he's shared the tough times, tedious times and the occasional humorous times. Others have died along the way. He'll miss them all. Once he leaves camp he'll be a deserter. Something he'll not be proud of, but if it means saving Spade, it's something he'll have to live with.

The night air is crisp. A slight breeze flutters the emu plume in his hat as he pokes his head out of the tent. There's only a quarter moon, but in the desert, it's enough to make most things visible. He sees only one sentry on guard. He's on his haunches with head down outside the temporary medic's tent. There would normally be more than one sentry around, but with the war over, so was the threat of an attack. Lewis banks on him being asleep and is about to run to the horses when a movement catches his eye.

Thinking the sentry has stirred, he retreats a little into his tent. But it's not the sentry. A small figure has emerged from the tent behind him. Lewis reckons it must be the girl saved during a post-war skirmish in a small Bedouin camp a few of days earlier. He was not involved but heard about it later.

Lewis watched with a niggling unease as she eases past the sleeping sentry then breaks into a run. *Bloody girl! She go bugger things up!* He wonders if he should alert the guard? *No!* Should he stop her? *Then do what? No!* It will mess up his plan to take Spade, and there'll be no other opportunity after this night. *Bugger it! Let her have her own escape. Not this fella's problem.* He watches her run towards the horse line. *If she scare 'em the whole bloody camp will wake up!* Unlike Lewis, the horses remain calm as she starts untying Spade. *Shit!*

It's only a twenty-five-yard dash, but before he can get to the corral, the girl has mounted the bareback Spade, spun him around with neck rope and rein in hand and kicked him into a gallop. Lewis only has time to grab the water bottle from under the saddle before giving chase. *No way she takin' my bloody horse.*

Despite his loping speed, Lewis can only watch as his horse disappears into the desert night. He'll continue to run until he can run no more, then, at first light, call on his tracking skills. He'll catch up and get his horse back no matter what.

[A'isha]

Alone in the darkened tent, A'isha hasn't taken her eyes of the guard who is just visible through a small gap in the tent flap. She'd noticed his lack of interest in her. *It must come with great shame to guard a simple young Bedouin girl rather than a Bedouin man.*

It's not long before his boredom turns to drowsiness. A'isha sits up as the sentry lowers himself onto his haunches. Slowly sliding off the stretcher bed, she watches with anticipation as his head nods a few times before resting his chin on his chest.

She removes the sling and flexes her arm to test its usability. There's some tolerable pain but she is pleased to have reasonable strength in her hand. On sandalled feet, she silently creeps to the tent flap and pokes her head out through the small gap. A cautious look to her left and right confirms there are no other guards. She delicately unties the flap tapes and slips out of the tent. A final check that the sentry is well asleep, then, without hesitation, she runs light-footed toward the horses. They remain calm. Her years herding goats have perfected the art of approaching animals without startling them.

The horse she had watched being generously watered and fed before nightfall is the chosen one. She unties the rope from the line, gives a reassuring pat on the horse's nose and a gentle stroke down its neck. With little effort, she pushes him back and away from the other horses. A snort, resulting in a cloud of condensed breath in the cold night air, is the horse's only reaction. In an instant, she's on his bare back, one hand holding the neck rope and the other a handful of mane. Both heads turn toward the desert and Spade is kicked into a gallop. *I am free. I am in my own terrain. I have rid me of the enemy.*

On instinct, she looks back and barely makes out the shape of a figure running after her. Is it the guard? *No matter, no man can catch a horse in full gallop.* Leaning forward over Spade's neck, she rips the bandage from her head. Her long dark hair now trails in the wind to match Spade's flowing mane. She'll ride as fast and as far as she can in the cool of night, for in the early morning, they'll need to find shelter from the sun's heat.

Chapter 4
THE FIRST NIGHT

Lewis' determination and simmering rage has fuelled him onward through most of the night. But tenacity and ire are not enough. His thin, wiry legs begin to cramp. His inherent stamina is fading. The tracks he has managed to follow are beginning to be swept away by swirling sand. Now cloud is masking the light from the moon and he submits to his body crying out for rest. He lowers himself to the ground, confident in his ability to pick up the tracks at first light. Sitting cross-legged, he stares into the darkness ahead and pictures his horse racing further away. His eyes close, allowing him to drift into Dreaming. A deep murmur blends with the soft ambient sound of shifting sand as he chants to the desert spirits for guidance. He hears his mother's reassuring voice repeat the lessons on tracking and outback survival skills.

During the past two years in combat, Lewis would sit, as he is now, drifting off into his spiritual mind. In the silent darkness of closed eyes, images of Dreamtime would appear. Images that have followed his people for thousands of years. The drawn-out murmur that rises from deep within would carry him over a sea of calm and prepare him for battle.

An uneasy feeling ripples through his body. A sense that this new challenge could be more perilous than any enemy he has faced in war.

At the first wash of light in the Eastern sky, Lewis lifts himself up from the sand. He allows himself a small sip of water while studying the terrain before him. The soft ambient light gives an inviting glow to the desert. That will soon change once the sun shows its face. What lies ahead is not all soft shifting sand as some deserts are, but a mix of sand and hard rocky ground. In an hour the sun will spread its heat, the horizon will shimmer, and all living things will have found shade. But not Lewis. Not until he catches up with Spade. *That girl, she Bedouin,* he reminds himself. *She'll look for shade and water and not put her ride at risk. That's when this fella will track'em down.*

He sets off in a determined stride, not fast, but steady. After only a short distance, he stops and looks back in the direction he came. The possibility that his regiment is out searching for him has crossed his mind. If they are, they'll have no problem catching him on horseback. He'll be charged with desertion, locked up and never see Spade again. He heads off in a direction other than where he wants to go. After a reasonable distance that should lead anyone following astray, he takes off his shirt so that it trails on the ground behind him. He backtracks in a wide arc to the point of his diversion leaving only swept ground in his wake. He takes a moment to re-focus on the direction calling him, then, with renewed vigour and trailing shirt erasing his tracks, he resumes the chase.

As if destined to be, he soon comes across the

familiar tracks of his horse. But the time taken sending any pursuers on the wrong course was time wasted. The sun is rising, and the heat is beginning to bite. Lewis puts his shirt back on. Pulls down his slouch hat to further shade his dark brown eyes and peers into the increasing heat haze ahead. In the distance, floating above the shimmering ground, he can make out the peak of a hill. *That girl, I bet she find shelter there.* His time in this country has taught him a lot about the Arabs and Bedouin. Now he must think like them. He quickens his pace with renewed anticipation.

As the sun continues to rise, Lewis finds himself struggling to keep a steady pace in the searing heat. Ahead, the mount appears no closer. He pauses for a sip of water and vows it will be his last until he finds his horse.

Peering over the raised water bottle, something in the distance catches Lewis' eye. The sun is reflecting off a shiny object. In the desert, this is not that common. Some rocks have a varnish-like coating of algae, but Lewis is sure this is metallic. Then, as if signalling its presence, the object projects an image of itself into the air. It's an image that Lewis recognises only too well. His heart skips a beat. Ignoring the heat; he runs towards his worst fear.

A horseshoe is lying on the sand with nails still attached. Lewis immediately recognises it's one of Spade's. He looks up and stares ahead with renewed intensity and fear for the condition of his horse. On this rocky ground and still some distance to the hill, a thrown shoe will do a lot of damage. He removes the nails and puts them in the button-down pocket of his pants for safe keeping.

The pockets are too small to carry a horseshoe, and it could fall from his grip if fatigue befuddles his mind. He removes one of his boot laces and chews it in half. One half is threaded back into some of the eyelets to secure the boot on his foot. The other half he threads into a nail hole each side the of the horseshoe. After tying the ends of the lace together, he hangs the horseshoe around his neck. As it thumps onto his chest a surge of energy from the metal shoe surprises him. A shiver runs down his sweating spine as a flash of intense power stings his mind.

[A'isha]

A'isha hardly remembers the last time she rode a horse. Riding one bareback is a new experience. If she were on a camel, she'd be sitting aside, not astride. Her straddling legs are now aching from tightly clinging on. Her grip on reins, rope and Spade's mane is also taking its toll on her injured arm. Despite being still bandaged, the shooting pain is becoming hard to bear. In her contrary manner, she refuses to believe keeping it in the sling would make any difference. *Just because the vulture looking Australian says so, no!*

Adding to her problems a sharp pain rebounds in her head with each stride of the horse, The gash on her temple begins to bleed. She lets go Spade's mane to wipe away the blood entering her eye. After several wipes, the bleeding eases, leaving her face smeared in red.

Regardless of her pain, the horse needs to rest. His breathing is heavy, he's lathered up, and he's beginning to stumble over the uneven ground. A'isha slides off Spade's back and urges him to lie down beside her without success. Any rest must be short for they need to get to the Djebel, still some distance away, before the sun rises. There they can shelter in the shade of the crevices and crags. With luck, they may even find water. She'd herded goats in similar hills to graze and drink from the pools of water left by the winter rains. But winter has long past, and water is not guaranteed.

*

A tug on the rope tied to her wrist stirs A'isha from an unintended sleep. Spade is restless as light begins to outline the horizon. Annoyed with herself, she must now hurry to get to the Djebel. She mounts Spade, nudges him with her sandalled feet and gets him up to full speed.

The ground has transformed into a firm crust. The rising sun casts shadows off the increasing number of pebbles, stones and rocks scattered over the sand. A'isha gives Spade a kick to his flanks to keep up the speed. A stumble on loose rocks almost dislodges her. She gives another kick, knowing shade and rest are not far away.

It soon becomes evident that Spade is not faring well. A'isha looks down and sees he's favouring his right foreleg. She dismounts for a closer examination. Not as familiar with horses as she is with shoeless goats, she overlooks the missing horseshoe. The leg flinches at her touch and Spade gives off a protesting whinny. Unsure what to do, she looks around for help that is not to be found. Accepting it unwise for the horse to carry her weight for fear it could make the leg worse, she'll lead him the rest of the way on foot.

The pace is slow as they're forced to follow a

meandering course around rocks and boulders of increasing size. The sun is now well clear of the horizon, dousing its rising heat on them as they finally reach the base of the Djebel. With Spade now limping badly, A'isha has to pull on the rope to keep him moving. They come across a shaded crevice surrounded by large boulders. An ideal place to stop and call on the goodness of the desert to show the way to water.

[Lewis]

Lewis is struggling against the intense heat. He has a raging thirst he refuses to quench. The sun's glare is blinding. The ground is now covered in pebbles and rocks making tracks harder to find let alone follow. The desperate need to seek shade now takes precedence. Following a trail will have to wait. He rushes towards the base of the hill, confident the girl and his horse will most likely be sheltering somewhere nearby.

As he reaches a shady overhang, a slight breeze carries with it an aroma. A familiar smell that has followed Lewis all his life…*horse shit!*

Drawn to the smell like a fly, it takes Lewis no time in coming across the welcoming brown parcel on the crusty ground. Diving in a hand tells him a lot. It's warm and moist. Spade is near. The surrounding crusted ground now exposes two fresh sets of tracks. To Lewis' trained eye, it's worryingly clear Spade is dragging the shoeless leg. It's enough for him to ignore the heat and fatigue. He sets off following the tracks around boulders and jagged outcrops. The erratic course can only do further harm. *Damn bloody girl! When you gunna stop?* He rounds a wind-scarred outcrop and into an area shaded by large boulders of limestone. Out of the sun's glare, his vision clears. There, tied to a rock, is Spade.

[A'isha]

Scrambling over, under and around large rocks and boulders, A'isha has yet to find water. Just as worrying is the increasing distance between her and the horse left tied to a rock. Just as she is about to give up all hope, she stumbles across the next best thing. At the base of one large limestone boulder is a tinge of green growth. With bare hands, she clears away a layer of pebbles and rests a hand on the sandy soil beneath. She feels a slight hint of dampness. With hopeful optimism, she seeks out a suitable piece of shale and begins to dig. The deeper the hole, the difference is the sound as the soil dampens until it's almost mud. A few more scoops and the first sign of murky water begins to seep to the surface. With nothing to carry water in, she'll need to bring the horse to it. By the time they come back, she reckons, the hollow should be full with settled water.

While elated with her find, the time it has taken has left her with an uneasy feeling. She rushes back to where she left the horse while mapping out a route that will be easier for it to travel over. Though weary, there's a spring in her step. The discovered water will allow her search for her family to continue.

In her eagerness to get the horse to water, she steps around a sloping ridge only to freeze on the spot. She quickly retreats. Her heart begins to pound. The horse is there where she left it. But so is a soldier!

Chapter 5
THE MEETING

[Lewis]

Lewis rushes to his horse ignoring the pain in his legs, his raging thirst and utter exhaustion. Spade backs away startled before realising who it is. He rears his head, stomps the ground and goes to meet his master only to be stopped short by the neck rope tied to a large rock.

"Stay!" Lewis calls out in a hushed tone to keep his horse calm "Steady down, mate."

He pushes Spade back to ease the strain on the rope. Spade sniffs the horseshoe hanging from Lewis' neck then rests his head on his shoulder. Lewis caresses his horse's neck, feeling the heat radiating from his body. Deep within he hears laboured breathing. He eases himself back, unscrews his water bottle, removes his hat and pours in the water, leaving a few drops to moisten his own cracked lips.

"What that bloody girl done to you, hey?" he whispers as Spade buries his nose into the hat. In no time all the water is gone leaving Spade nodding for more. "Sorry mate, that's all I got."

He removes the horseshoe hanging from his neck, puts his hat back on and begins to examine his horse. Finding no injuries to the bulk of his body, he bends back the right foreleg leg to check the shoeless hoof. The extent of damage adds further to his rage. He darts a glance up and around with fire in his eyes and mutters a curse on the girl for allowing this to happen.

Spade flinches with the removal of every embedded grain of sand and pebble from the soft frog of his hoof. The heat coming from the inflamed leg adds to Lewis' concern. He puts it down to bruising of the inside the hoof wall and the sooner he can make his horse more comfortable the better both will feel.

"This fella fix you up good and proper, you bet!"

He puts the thrown shoe to one side. Takes the nails from his pocket and examines them. Some are in need straightening. Easy if he had his tool bag that lies with everything else back at the camp. The limestone boulders appear hard enough to use as a base, but finding something to use as a hammer is another matter. There are rocks aplenty, but most are sandstone and crumble after only one or two blows. Even fragments of limestone break after several blows with only the slightest impact on the shape of each nail. All this is taking far too long, and Lewis still needs to look for water before it gets dark. He takes off his shirt to cool down and picks up speed.

With nails far from perfect but usable, Lewis sits exhausted and removes his boots and socks. He bends Spade's damaged leg back to hold it between his legs. He folds one woollen sock and pushes it gently into the recess of the hoof to cover the corium and cushion the frog. The other sock is stretched over the whole foot to hold the packing in place. He positioned the thrown shoe over the sock, and, with a supply of rocks gathered beside him, nails it back on.

Satisfied he's done all he can for the moment, Lewis puts his boots back on over bare feet. He'd prefer not to wear them, but since being in the army, his feet have softened. It'll take a moment for Spade to get used to his new padded hoof, allowing Lewis the opportunity for a short rest before their search of water.

[A'isha]

A'isha unsettled some stones in her haste to hide. With breath held and heart pounding, she waits for the sound of approaching footsteps. After a moment of welcome silence, she releases her breath and peers out from her cover. The soldier appears not to have seen or heard her. *Or does he consider the horse more important?* Looking past the soldier and around amazes her. *He has no horse. He is alone.* The memory of a figure chasing after her as she fled the camp flashes before her. *Is he the one?*

Rattled, A'isha crouches down with her tunic-covered knees tucked under her chin. She pulls her headscarf low over her head to gather her thoughts.

These foreign soldiers are not only dangerous but stupid. To follow me all this way into the desert on foot is foolish.

But what to do now he has the horse?

I can survive in the desert, but I cannot travel far on foot. I need the horse to help me find my family. But he? He has the horse and could make it back to his camp. But what of water? One thing I have learnt about these mounted soldiers is the care they give their horses. He will not risk the journey back to his camp without water on a horse that has a sore leg. There is still some hours before the heat dies down. I have water, so I can wait. But wait for what?

A'isha stands and chances another look. The soldier is examining the horse. Running a hand from his head, down his neck, his back, his rump and rear legs. He pauses with a hand on the horse's chest and an ear to his side. He then slides his hand down the flinching right foreleg. After a close examination of the shoeless hoof, he shoots a glance in A'isha's direction. She sees the rage in his bloodshot eyes.

Immediately she retreats into her hiding place and again waits for an approaching footfall. Again, none comes. Without certainty she was not seen, A'isha decides to sit and wait for the soldier to make the next move.

As time passes, A'isha drifts into a false calm. Suddenly she's alerted by the echoing sound of rock on rock. Startled, yet curious, she sneaks a look. Satisfied the soldier has his mind on other things, she watches with puzzled interest as the soldier continues to pound something on a large rock with smaller rocks that break one after the other. This prolonged, concentrated process allows A'isha to study her pursuer in greater detail. Now shirtless and sweating, the first thing that intrigues her is the colour of his skin and his lean, shiny body. *He is not like other soldiers I have seen. If he wore a long, loose thobe and sandals instead of pants and boots, he would pass as an Arab. Of course, his hat with its feather would need to go.*

Seeing the soldier beside the horse stirs a recollection. *He is the one I watched from my prison bed watering and feeding the horse. I now understand he wanting his horse back. Such a horse of Arab breeding is of great value and a worthy gift for an important Sheikh.*

Chapter 6
THE WATER HOLE

[A'isha]

A'isha's fury is soothed somewhat by her cultural belief that rage is poison to one's capability to think straight.

She chances a look over the rocky ridge. The soldier is concentrating on tending to his horse. She notes his dedication, then is intrigued when he removes his socks and does what he does with them. His lean, dark body glistens with sweat, reminding her of another time when she spied on a young man. He was of her tribe, and his good looks and chiselled body long infatuated her. One day, while on her way to collect water, she came across him bathing at the well. Believing he did not see her, she hid behind a clump of date palms. If he sensed she was watching he didn't show it, nor worry that she was. In fact, he kept washing his body for much longer than was necessary. So strong was the impression it had on her that she believed the day would come when they would marry. A dream dashed when her father informed her that he had arranged for a bloated and ageing Sheikh from a distant tribe to be her husband. No matter how rich or powerful or what the marriage would bring to her family, it was not at all what she had fantasised.

But there was no such fantasising at the sight of a semi-naked foreign enemy. All she wants from him is his horse. *He has replaced the lost shoe that I regret I did not notice. Did he come across it, or did he bring one with him? No matter, for he has tended to the injured horse for me. I have patience, and I have water. Chance will come when I will once again claim the horse as my own and continue on my journey.*

[Lewis]

Lewis feels drowsiness wash over him, but sleep is not a luxury time will allow. He slaps himself across the cheeks, stands and readjusts his hat. Finding water cannot wait.

The terrain is different to the vast plains of the Australian outback. There, Spinifex and shrubs give a hint of moisture in the ground. But all Lewis can see in front of him is flat crusty ground covered by fluvial gravel and nothing but sand beyond. There are no trees, therefore no wadis as far as the eye can see. At his back is the Djebel, a towering mound of sandstone, limestone and layers of shale sandblasted into crevices and hollows. Not at all promising, but surely water must be hiding somewhere. Then it dawns on him. *That girl…where is she? No way she tie Spade to a rock for him to die…no bloody way!* He looks around with alert eyes and ears primed. *She gone look for water, I bet. She Bedouin…she know how to find water in this place.* His experienced eye locks onto disturbed rocks and soft impressions in the ground. He looks ahead to where the tracks lead. A smile stretches his cracked lips then evaporates just as quick. *But,* he asks himself looking around, *I bet she watch from some place. Wait for me to go then grab Spade again? No, he come with me.*

[A'isha]

A'isha cowers deeper into the crevice as the soldier leads the horse towards her. Her dark clothes merge into the shadow. Her headscarf is pulled across her face, leaving only her dark brown eyes uncovered. She crouches down into a tight ball to lessen her size and watches them pass. Her relief at not being discovered soon changes to anguish as they head in the direction of her water hole.

No! I cannot allow him to find my water. If I had my father's dagger, I would jump on his back and slit his throat.

But, with no dagger, all she can do is control her unease, wait till they are far enough away, then follow from a distance.

[Lewis]

Lewis stops and pulls Spade to a halt. Thinking he'd heard something, he turns back to listen. All has gone quiet. He continues for a short distance and stops again. All is quiet, but the feeling of being followed is strong. *That no animal, lizard or snake. It girl, I bet.* A sharp tug on the rope in his hand breaks his concentration. Despite a sore leg and rough ground, Spade takes off dragging Lewis with him towards the smell of water. All attempts at pulling up his horse or steering him towards smoother ground fail. Before long, Spade has his head down into the freshly dug hole filled to the brim with muddy water. Lewis tightens his grip on the rope and looks around, convinced this is the work of the Bedouin girl. *I bet she around somewhere watching. Bloody pissed off I found her water, too, I bet. She be okay for the horse drink, though.* For a satisfying moment, a smile of retribution loosens his lips. *She took my horse. Now I take her water.*

[A'isha]

A'isha watches from a ledge overlooking her waterhole. Her fingers dig into the sandstone turning her knuckles white. Whatever hatred she had for the foreign enemy soldier has turned into uncontrolled rage. She dug the hole with her bare hands and found the water. It is her water, even though, by the law of the desert, it is free to share with all…but not this foreign enemy soldier!

Forcing herself to calm down, she assesses the reality of the situation. *It must have taken great effort to catch up to me on foot. Then all the hard work putting the shoe back on the horse. All without rest. He will now settle down by my waterhole to wait for the sun to set. That is when his will to stay awake will fade. I too am tired, but I have not run through the night, and I am used to watching over my goats without sleep. So I will think of him, and his horse, as my goats and watch and wait. He has mended the horse to be fit to ride again. Yes, drink my water beloved horse, for you will soon have me on your back once again.*

[Lewis]

Spade has consumed all the water that had seeped into the hollow. It will fill again for Lewis to drink. He settles down on the ground with his back propped up against a rock to wait. Spade slurps up the last of the water then gives a half-satisfied snort and a shake of the head that tugs on the neck rope now tied to Lewis' left ankle. Lewis is beginning to feel drowsy. He pulls on the rope to bring Spade closer. Spade gives another shake of the head, a disagreeable sneeze to rid his nostrils of mud then lowers his head for Lewis to stroke.

Lewis looks around at the lengthening shadows. In a couple of hours, the sun will start to set, and the heat will melt into darkness. He'll then check if Spade is fit enough to walk through the night. But to where? And in what direction? It needs to be a place with shade and water when the sun rises. Any thought of returning to the camp is dismissed. No, he must keep going to a place where they can stay together. He searches his memory for the most recent map he'd seen. Where the last camp was set up, the coast lay to the North. As he headed into the rising sun to reach this mound, then he must head to the right of the setting sun. With a full water bottle, they should at least make it to the rail line at Birel Abd before the heat of the new day. There, they can get water from the pipeline that runs beside the rails. Where there is a water pipeline, there is usually vegetation. And where there is water and vegetation, there is usually some form of life…edible life. Which, right now, is desperately needed.

Chapter 7
THE EVIL EYE

[A'isha]

Patience in the desert is good. In fact, according to Bedouin belief, it's deemed to be the 'beautiful patience'. Maybe, but there comes a time to act upon the reason for such patience. A'isha has watched the horse have its fill of water. Now is the time to make her move. Now is the time to test her power. *You, enemy soldier, will need to wait for the hole to fill with enough water to drink before risking another chase. By then I will be so far into my desert you will never catch me!*

A'isha focusses her mind on the drowsy Lewis with increasing intensity. Her eyes redden with strain and the pain in her head erupts again. She touches the amulet around her neck. For what she is about to do she will need all her faith in its protection.

You, infidel enemy, I see you as an impure dog, and unlike a blue-eyed ram, your brown eyes will not save you from the Evil Eye I cast upon you.

Sweat beads her forehead, stinging her wound. She grasps the three parcels of her talisman tightly and clenches her teeth. Her eyes become frozen in a fierce stare. She will not blink until she is sure her spell is cast.

What little water there is seeping into the hollow, ripples from a silent tremor. Loose pebbles dance unseen by the human eye. A sandgrouse pokes its head out from its sandy burrow. Above, a disturbed Lanner Falcon takes flight. A Sinai agama lizard scurries over a rock showing a confused out-of-season tinge of blue. A rumble of thunder in a cloudless sky sends it and all other creatures scurrying back to where they came from. Overhead the falcon is circling in tighter and tighter spirals creating a mini twister of rising dust. Spade shuffles and jerks his head back with ears pricked. A pull on the rope tied to Lewis' leg stirs him out of his drowsiness. He sits up, expecting to catch the girl making a grab for his horse. All he sees is the spiral of dust swirling around him only to fade back into the ground at his feet. His legs cramp up as he struggles to stand for a better look around. His stomach tightens, his head begins to spin, his eyelids flicker and his vision blurs. He reaches out to Spade for support, but the pain now spreading through his body and the swirling dizziness in his head force him to drop to his knees. Spade shuffles out of the way as Lewis' limp body crashes to ground…facing the waterhole…and a black-necked cobra that had come to drink. The startled snake raises its head, and with a slight jerk forward, spits a spray of venom into Lewis's flickering eyes.

It's the last thing the cobra will ever do as Spade plunges his newly shod hoof onto the back of its head, splitting it open and staining the already red earth.

[A'isha]

When A'isha was old enough to realise she had no voice, she felt it was for a reason. Taken and replaced with something else. She studied everyone she came across and accepted, apart from no voice, she was normal. But, in doing so, everyone she studied, studied her back. Could they see what had replaced her voice, she wondered? When her mother made talismans for her and others in her family to wear it aroused her suspicions.

Her cultural education included the spirits of the desert and the Djinn. The possibility she may have some power was never tested. It was not from want but fear. Fear of the unknown. Fear the tattoo of her forehead meant something bad. Fear of being cast aside. Fear of losing the young man she spied on at the wadi.

Did she really have the power or the gift to cast an Evil Eye on someone? This was to be her first test. So, it was a bit of surprise to see her enemy soldier actually succumb. But the biggest surprise was the cobra. Not expected, nor wished for. All she wanted was for the soldier to sleep long enough for her to flee on his horse.

Oh, masters of the desert, what have I done? The power you have given me was not meant to be so strong. I have seen desert foxes become victim to the cobra's venom and I do not wish that on anyone…not even my worst enemy.

Her teachings on desert survival covered a multitude of possible dangers. The effects caused by cobra venom, and what action to take, is near the top of the list. If the venom is not washed from the eyes quickly, the victim will be permanently blind!

Realising the seriousness is cause for A'isha to question her action.

What has this soldier done to me? Nothing! It is I who stole his horse. Why would he not want to get it back?

By all that is holy, please forgive me for what I have done.

She rushes to his side.

[Lewis]

If it was a snake bite, Lewis knew what to do. He's been bitten more than once, but never spat at. The confusion of a dulled spinning head, semi-paralysed body and now instant painful blindness causes him to panic. He gropes around for something, anything to wipe or even scrape away the stinging attack on his eyes.

Spade has seen his share of snakes and has put many out of their existence, but then he would watch whoever was bitten treat themselves. But this is different, and even to a horse, a confused sense of helplessness. Suddenly, a movement to his side startles him. Fearing another snake, Spade stutters and backs up, pulling on the rope still tied to Lewis' leg. Lewis feels the tug and reaches down for it with one hand, while the other continues to grope at his eyes. No matter how great the pain is and the sheer panic of blindness, he will not be separated from his horse.

[A'isha]

The water hole is now the centre of utter chaos. A horrified mute girl, a blinded young soldier and a confused and panicked horse. A'isha needs to tend to Lewis fast, but Spade is in a protective mood. She approaches him as calm as her inner frenzy will allow and gently strokes Spade's neck. Their eyes meet. A residue of her recently discovered power quietens Spade enough to allow her some space.

She kneels down and pushes the flattened body of the snake aside to clear access to the water hole. With some hesitation, she touches Lewis' shoulder; a touch that would never be allowed in her camp. But this was now her camp and the soldier was now her responsibility. She feels Lewis flinch at her touch. If she could only speak she would calm him with her words, but silence is her communication, and she touches his shoulder again.

[Lewis]

Lewis' mind is spinning. His body begins to shake uncontrollably. Despite the trauma of not knowing what is happening, he manages to pull on the rope. Spade lowers his head, and Lewis feels hot breath on his face. The comfort this gives him allows the second touch on his shoulder to stay. He lets go the rope and reaches out for whoever is there. Not knowing if it's the girl or someone else does not matter. He needs help.

"Who's there?" he calls out then strains to hear a reply. But there is none. "Is that you girl?" Again there is no answer. The only response is a hand on his other shoulder, and his unresponsive body dragged a short distance. One hand is released while the other moves to the back of his head and gently pushes it down. The splash of water on his face startles him but is cooling.

Another splash and another follow. He blinks to allow the water to flush out whatever was spat at him. But with each blink his panic grows. No matter if his eyes are open or closed, it's all the same…total darkness.

[A'isha]

If I could talk it would be a waste as our language is different. I can only show my regret by a comforting touch and the urgency in washing the poison from your eyes.

A'isha feels a nudge in the back from Spade as if urging her on to heal his friend.

If I can wash away all the poison in time, I may also win the horse's friendship.

Did I mean 'also'? Do I really want to be friends with this foreigner? I may not hate him as much now, but to befriend one who imprisoned me? I do not think so. I will do my best to bring back his sight, then…?

A'isha removes the bandage from her arm and waits for more water to seep into the hole. She looks at her injured arm for the first time. It's bruised and swollen, and now without the firm binding aches.

She allows the seeping water to saturate the bandage then wipes Lewis' eyes and face. After several goes, she ties the freshly soaked bandage around Lewis' head and over his eyes. For now, it is all she can do. The pain in his eyes will ease, but sight will take longer to come back…if indeed it does! Will she grab this opportunity to steal the horse and leave him? The thought is tempting.

It would be easy to untie the rope from his ankle and ride off. There is water. He made it this far from his camp. I'm sure he could make it back when some sight returns. I will stay with him until the sun goes down but no longer. I'll take his water bottle. A problem he will need to sort out. But my freedom is more important.

[Lewis]

The disorientation Lewis felt before being blinded is easing, but the pain in his eyes remains just as intense. The panic of sudden blindness has taken away any thought of what to say. He's certain the girl is washing his eyes. But he wonders why she has not said anything, even in a language he may not understand. He's picked up a few words of Arabic. Words overheard by others in his battalion…words that were regrettably not that endearing towards the Arabs.

He tightens his grip on Spade's rope. If he is to remain blind, Spade will take him back to the camp. Unfortunately, Spade will be giving up his own life as an unfair reward for his act of loyalty.

The pain and fear of blindness make any plans irrelevant until he can think straight. And that is becoming difficult. A night's chase, a day's walk in the hot sun, no sleep and the events of the day leading up to this moment, are sending Lewis into unconsciousness.

"Spade?" he utters in a feeble voice. Again he feels Spade's breath on the side of his face. The neck rope loosens in his hand. He pulls it with the last of his fading strength to reassure himself the other end is tied to his ankle. "Spade, stay with me big fella. Don't bloody leave, hey, no matter what." A nudge and a snort from his horse's nose is enough for Lewis to allow sleep to wash over him.

Chapter 8
A ROPE A KNOT AND SPIRITS

[A'isha]

Everything about this soldier she examines. His skin, his hair, his smell, his clothes, his possessions. All judged and compared to what she has grown up with. She studies and smells his army issue water bottle before filling it with water. It's so different to the sheep's bladder she always used. And after some consideration, one she still prefers.

Despite whatever she prefers, it would have no effect on the quality of the water. The seepage is slow, and the constant claiming water to keep the bandage wet allows no time for it to settle. She'll rely on the bandage to filter the water before seeping through into his eyes. *With the will of Allah—or whoever this foreign soldier worships — the snake's poison should be washed away.*

A'isha looks around at the cramped, shady space they all occupy while waiting for more water to appear. Spade has taken up the majority of space by lying on the rocky ground with his head resting on Lewis' legs—a common arrangement during lapses in battle. His bulk and the need to keep the water hole clear allows room for little else. Each move A'isha makes has Spade lift his head in a constant vigil of his companion.

The Bedouin have a high regard for loyalty. A'isha will put that to the test when daylight fades, the temperature drops and she unties the rope to lead the horse away. Until then, she will keep applying water to avert permanent blindness. *If the gods are on his side, he should have some sight back in the following night. Then, he will be able to make it back to his camp.*

*

With the temperature dropping and light fading in the sky, A'isha decides to make her move. After one more drizzle of water over the bandage, she gently strokes Lewis' forehead to test he's asleep. He moves, but she believes it's a nightmarish pain swirling around in his head. She slides her hand from his forehead, over his bare sweat-covered shoulder and down his bare arm. She pauses momentarily to study his tight muscles and thinks of the boy in her tribe and how she desires to stroke his arm. *Will I ever get that chance? A question unanswered until Allah determines my fate.*

Lewis' relaxed grip on the rope makes it easy for A'isha to slide it from his fingers. A slight groan murmurs from his open lips. She pauses. She goes to untie the knot around his ankle. The soldier may be asleep, but his horse is not, and the rope runs under its resting head. A'isha repositions herself and runs her fingers through Spade's mane to keep him calm. She's rarely frustrated by having no voice, but now would be one of those times when a soft whisper in a horses ear would be useful. Spade lifts his head enough to release the rope. The knot tied to Lewis' ankle comes apart with little resistance. Keeping a watchful eye on Lewis, she slides the rope from under his leg and gathers it up with the reins.

She pulls evenly on the rope as she stands, urging Spade to follow. Spade looks up at her and wrenches back the rope and reins. Bared teeth stop her grabbing them back. Again she tries, but this time Spade snatches them back with his teeth and rests his head back onto Lewis.

Your loyalty is commendable, dear horse, but you owe me for saving your master from blindness. For that, you must show me some loyalty.

All the movement stirs Lewis, but not enough to fully wake him. He starts to make noises like a mob of buzzing insects.

Is he singing to himself?

It reminds her of the dirges she has heard in other Bedouin camps.

Is this a sign we are to die here? No, I will not let that happen. He can sing as much as he likes, but I will not follow him to extinction.

As she thinks of another way to take control of the horse, a grumbling noise emanates from Spade's stomach. *Water will keep you alive, dear horse, but food is what will get you on your feet.*

The moss at the base of the rock showed the way to water, but will not feed a horse. A'isha silently creeps away. Spade lifts his head and watches till she's out of sight. Satisfied she is no longer a threat; he rests his head back down.

A'isha would herd her flock of goats to similar rocky areas. They would munch on the spring growth sprouting from dust that has blown in and settled around the rocks and crevices. Such can be the picture of glorious colour that brings the desert to life. But this is not spring. If any plants have managed to get a foothold, they would be in the shady cracks and crevices. Out of the heat and waiting for the rain to come.

[Lewis]

Blinded by lingering pain, a dose of snake venom and a damp rag covering his eyes, Lewis' mind is wandering into a Dreamtime state. Images of his cultural spirits appear in the haze of his imagination. Or, is it imagination? He has known of Dreamtime spirits being forces that go beyond the mind. Belief in them remains as strong as the day of their first telling.

The air is still around the waterhole, but inside Lewis' mind is a whirlwind of totemic ancestors swirling around in all their various forms. They are the creators of his world—a world thousands of miles away. They created the layout of the land. The hills and trees, the rivers and lakes and all creatures that live off that land. Parrots, Emus, Wallabies and Kangaroos, transport his presence back to his homeland…his land…his songline…as decreed by his elders for him alone. A closely held secret that will never change until he releases his spirit from his physical body. But there is a disturbing conflict. This is not his homeland. This is not a place crisscrossed by thousands of songlines of his people. It is a foreign land— but a land indeed created. Created by the cultural spirits of the people that live here. The same spirits that have created their own unique landscape, flora and fauna. This inevitably means they…the indigenous Bedouin… must have their own songlines.

Chapter 9
DARKNESS IN THE DAY

[A'isha]

Clambering over rocks and boulders has left A'isha weary and footsore. The search for food has taken far too long. Her meagre harvest consists of some dried twigs, a bunch of desert thistle, a handful of other plants with their roots still attached—something she regrets for it's best to leave the roots so others can feed on the growth that springs from them—a dozen or more crickets that were feasting on the plants, three slightly squashed scorpions, a variety of flattened spiders of considerable size, and some other creepy-crawlies found under rocks. Not much considering the time it has taken. She came across some mice and lizards, but A'isha is never a good hunter of things with fur or bigger than an insect. The plants and roots are for the horse, including the thistle with their sharp thorns. She knows camels eat them but is unsure if a horse has the same leathery mouth. *I'll keep the insects for myself. The soldier can have the dead cobra. A small offering, but enough, I feel, to get the horse and myself through the night.*

The air is refreshingly cooler. The half moon is providing ample light for her to continue her interrupted journey. Her mind fills with images of those she misses and hopes to find soon. She arrives back at the waterhole with a sense of accomplishment and favourable prospects. In an instant, all her hopes and expectations disappear into an unwelcome void…as empty as the area where the soldier and the horse should be.

Her heart skips a beat. She looks around in a panic. *Did I lose my way? No! There is the water hole. There is the dead snake. It's not my way I lost…it's my ride!*

[Lewis]

The Dreamtime stories that swirl around inside Lewis' head and heart carry him back to his country. Back among his people. Back in the outback desert where every plant, animal, insect and reptile is familiar. Most of all, back in the saddle of his horse. A faint smile softens his pained expression as the thunder of running cattle, and the crack of a bullwhip is as it should be. But the dream is suddenly blown away. The pain in his eyes is not meant to be, nor the mask he's wearing. He frantically rips away the bandage and painfully opens his eyes. The shock of blindness is definitely not meant to be.

Waking from darkness into more darkness has rattled Lewis' mind. The years of battles come flooding back. Bloodied lifeless bodies with vacant stares appear to walk over him. Their magnetism is urging him to follow. Is he dying? Or, is he already dead? He reaches his arms out in a confused panic. Is he trying to stop them taking his soul, or is he begging them to allow him to follow?

Spade lifts his head from Lewis' legs and comes in contact with a waving hand. A flash of memory invades

Lewis' delirium. His horse has not left him. He runs a hand over Spade's nose, his headcollar and traces the leather back stay to the attached rope. Like a flickering light bulb attempting to glow, he tries to picture what has happened.

Lewis slides out from under Spade and begins to explore the area by feel. He recoils as his hand lands on the snake. He expects a reaction from Spade if it were alive. There is none. He examines by blind touch the distorted dead body. Certain it was the work of Spade, he reaches back to give him a stroke of appreciation. Spade is still lying down. A shiver ripples down Lewis' spine. Has the snake bitten his horse? Unable to examine him by sight, the only way to find out is to get Spade on his feet.

Getting to his own feet is an effort. His head starts to spin. Giddy and disorientated, Lewis loses his balance and drops down with one arm immersed in water. *The waterhole!* Like a reminding tap on the shoulder, scraps of reality become clearer. *Yes, the water hole, cast shoe, bent nails, bruised hoof, his socks…and the Bedouin girl.*

He reaches back, takes hold of the neck rope and strains to listen.

"Girl, you there?"

There is only the whisper of a gentle breeze.

"You no be afraid, hey. This fella not hurt you." Not that he could in his blind state.

"You bloody silly bugger take my horse…but this fella forgive."

The continuing silence has him worried.

"Whatever you did to my eyes, me forgive you for

that too, but think about it…we need each other, hey?"

He traces the neck rope to a rock solidly embedded in the ground. Did he tie it there in his blind confusion? He unfastens it and knots it around his wrist. It's now more important than ever to have his horse close by in his new and frightening world of darkness.

His thoughts return to the snake and Spade. Despite another bout of dizziness, he manages to get his feet. A tug on the rope and Spade immediately follows. A relieved Lewis needs a moment to quell his feeling of nausea. He leans on Spade with an arm over his back and his head resting on his side. The sound of internal rumbling brings another reality. "You hungry, boy? Me too. Last meal back at camp, hey?" But Lewis is not sure how long ago that was. The air has cooled so it must be night. "Was it the night before we left camp, Spade? Or has this silly bugger been asleep long time?

But it is night and night is when to travel in the desert. Lewis considers his options. They're not that encouraging.

That girl, she no leave without Spade. No, she around somewhere. Gone do private business, maybe. But she come back and take Spade for sure, and I not see to stop her. No, we go now while she away.

Short on confidence, Lewis accepts he'll need to fend for himself…somehow. Food is something that can wait. It'll not be the first time they've travelled hungry; such was warfare in the desert. And then there's Spade's injured hoof. Lewis feels his way to the stressed leg. It still trembles at his touch. Further examination will have to be by feel only. He presses his thumb and forefinger together behind the bruised hoof. The heat has subsided and the swelling feels like it's gone down a bit, but Spade remains unfit to ride.

Lewis kneels down and reaches into the water hole to feel its depth. With cupped hand, he splashes water into his open eyes. All it offers is some cooling, but no light. Spade shuffles out of the way and watches Lewis pat the ground until he locates his water bottle. He fills it, takes a long drink and fills it again. Less successful is the search for his hat. It's not so much for him to wear, but for Spade to drink from. He manages to stand and waits for his head to once again clear. But the pain remains.

He puts on the shirt still wrapped around his waist. Then runs a hand over his belt, down his pants, over his leggings and to his boots where he tightens the laces. A habit of checking his uniform instilled in him since his training. He places the leather strap of the water bottle over a shoulder and across his chest. A hand raises to check his hat then remembers he can't find it.

Spade now needs to drink as much water as he can. He pulls on the rope to direct him to the water only to have it wrenched out of his hand. Lewis hears his horse shuffle away and freezes, thinking another snake is about or the girl. Instead, Spade returns with a nudge to his back. Something tickles him, and Lewis blindly explores. Clasped between Spade's teeth is the lost hat, its emu plume shivering in the breeze against his arm. Lewis puts it on and lowers Spade's head to the water.

Lewis uses the time while Spade drinks to position himself in his last remembered location. One of his tracking skills is his ability to sense direction. An inbuilt compass if you like. But even if he knew in which direction to head, could he stay on that course? The lack of sight meant no moon or stars to guide him, but he still had the sense of smell and the feel of a breeze. He remembers the breeze that carried the odour of Spade's dung came from the East. He needs to head north towards the coast. If the breeze he now feels has not changed direction, it should then kiss his right cheek. It's a big ask to rely on all the uncertainties and trusting the breeze to keep blowing from the same direction. Once Spade has his fill, there is no time to waste, for Lewis has no idea if the night has just started or is about to end.

It only takes a few steps to face reality. The rocky ground would be hard to traverse for a sighted person, but for a blind man, it's almost impossible. Unless he can find a smoother route, Spade's injured hoof will worsen. Lewis could also stumble and twist or break a leg. Accepting it's too dangerous to continue, Lewis is about to return to the water hole. But Spade has a clearer view of their situation. He takes up the slack of the rope and sets off in the lead.

[A'isha]

It is said by those wiser than me, that a live man is more useful than a dead one. If this man comes with the horse, then so be it.

A'isha devours as much water as she can stomach. She soaks the discarded rag once wrapped around Lewis' eyes. It's her only way of carrying, at least, a little water. She adds the dead snake to her food supply.

Under the moonlight, A'isha has no trouble following

the trail of the blind, stumbling soldier. Before long they both come into view.

I will follow from a distance without them knowing. Then at the time of Allah's choosing, I will take control of the horse. If I am met with resistance, I will offer them the food I carry. Their hunger will not allow them to reject such a generous offer. That would most certainly put them in my debt, and they would then follow in the direction of my choosing.

[Lewis]

With Spade leading, travel is slow but steady. The ground is becoming less rock and more sand. The breeze is getting stronger yet still whistling in Lewis' right ear. Only once did he need to pull on the rope to keep Spade heading north. Since then, he has not deviated from that direction. Relying on the long-standing trust he has for his horse, Lewis can relax a little while the pain in his eyes eases.

Chapter 10
SILENT DARKNESS

[Lewis]

Back in Australia, he would walk through the night following the spirits of his ancestors. Images of their form would create a breeze swirling around him. Their song would lift him till his feet felt they had left the earth. He would then float along the songline. He was never alone. Nor was he now. Beside Spade, he knew he had company. It's clear to him the Bedouin girl is following.

"She strange one that one," he utters to his horse who has a quick glance around on hearing Lewis voice. "I know she there but why she not catch up, hey?"

After a few more steps on the uneven ground, he adds, "Better she not, hey. Not to be trusted that girl. Rob me of you again, I bet."

But the thought she is following provokes Lewis to be more sensitive to his unseen surroundings.

Sound has become Lewis' most relied on sense, but he struggles to hear further than the ground under their feet. The cacophony of his boots and Spade's metal shoes knocking, crushing and sliding over a mix of sand, pebbles and rocks drown out all other sounds.

Lewis delves deeper into his blackness. His lack of sight elevates his concentration. He begins to peel away each layer of prominent sound. First is the constant underlying squeaking of sand under each footstep. It allows other sounds to enter that he must identify. He pats the back of Spade. The surrounding sounds begin to define themselves. A brush of his hand over Spade's back is faint but noted. The quickness of his breathing is worrying, but clear. Lewis lifts his head, reaching out for sounds further afield. The rustle of padded feet is faint. Possibly a desert fox hunting for prey.

He tries harder to find other layers of sound, then stops.

While pleased with his effort, it has distracted him from the another important sense. One that he has been relying on…his sense of touch. The breeze that has directed his progress is no longer kissing his right cheek, but brushes against the other side of his face. He is no longer heading to the coast but deeper into the desert.

A rush of panic washes over him and he pulls on the rope to halt Spade. His mind starts spinning with calculations. How long has deciphering the sounds preoccupied him? How far have they gone before he noticed? Or, worse still, has the wind changed direction?

Lewis spins around in a fit of panic. Whichever direction he faces, the breeze follows him. He raises a hand hoping his sweating palm will give a more accurate sense of the wind's direction. Like a weather vane, he twists his hand to feel the coolest effect of the wind. Gyrating it back and forward, he gradually locks onto its strongest influence. He turns his head, so the right side of his face once again meets with the breeze. But his inner instinct is telling him this is no longer the direction he should be heading. He sniffs the air in the faint hope of picking up the remotest whiff of the Mediterranean Sea. All he can smell is sand in his nostrils.

The stars and moon shine brightly overhead offering guidance, but Lewis only sees the blackest of black. He now has no idea in which direction to head. Spade shakes his head with a whinny.

"You have as much idea as me, mate," Lewis confesses. "This bloody stupid black fella now got us lost."

Another shake of his head and Spade begins to walk. The rope tightens in Lewis' hand.

"Okay, big fella. You the one with eyes."

[A'isha]

A'isha had relied on blindness and lack of sleep to render the soldier immobile. She was wrong. Wrong also in not accepting the fact that she too had not slept for just as long. The soldier had collapsed and so slept while she searched for food. Now fatigue is draining her strength. The cache of food she carries seems heavier. And, despite the slowness of the two ahead, the distance between them is widening. If she loses sight of the two, she can still follow their tracks, but she's beginning to wonder. Does this soldier know where he is going? He cannot see so why are the tracks changing direction?

An attempt to quicken her pace loosens her grip on the hem of her thobe. The food cradled in the fold spills out over the ground. By the time she gathers up the spilt load, the soldier and horse are out of sight.

A rush of fear ripples through her. She has never been entirely alone in the desert before. There was

always company, even if it be just goats, the odd camel…
or a soldier's horse.

*I cannot lose myself in loneliness. I cannot allow it. I
have my beliefs and spirits to accompany me. I must sing
in my head and let those who protect me sing along with
me. I will gather more voices as I go. Then I will have my
own desert caravan of friendly souls.*

[Lewis]

Lewis' mind is starting to meander in the sea of
opaque blackness. Thoughts of getting lost and dying
in the desert stir memories of Lewis' far-off home. His
mother and those who returned from walkabout passed
down their stories of his mob's culture. They taught him
to dance as a young boy. They would smear him with
body paint, stick a feather in the back of his loincloth
and teach him how to dance like an emu. The memory
of stiff arm movements and plenty of ground stomping
resonates through to his boots. He allows himself a skip
and a stomp…much to the surprise of Spade. The crunch
and rattling of rocks underfoot fade. Lewis allows the
breathing music of the didgeridoo and the brittle sound
of clapping sticks to carry him home.

A tear adds to his blind, weeping eyes as he accepts
he will never see his mother again. Even if he survives, he
cannot return to Australia. But memories are unleashed.
Thoughts of his father are mixed. He didn't even know
the man he saw riding and running the station was his
father for maybe six years. Even then, it was four more
years before he had contact with him. He was a hard
master and while in his presence, Lewis was to act like

a white man. This confused the young Lewis. For it was stressed that beyond the walls of the homestead, he was nothing more than an Aboriginal stockman.

Of course, this was what Lewis preferred to be. By nature, with his mob. But there were times when his father invited him indoors. One occasion brings a smile to his parched lips. After downing a glass of whisky to toast Queen Victoria, his father, being an eternally proud Scot, would don his tartan beret, beckon the young Lewis to sit on his knee and sing him a Scottish ditty.

It was made up of words he never did understand, but he knew then off by heart. To the rhythm of their steady gait, Lewis begins to hum the sound of a didgeridoo. Then, in full voice, breaking the silence of the desert, and a startled reaction from Spade, he sings.

> *HAME came our goodman,*
> *And hame came he,*
> *And then he saw a saddle-horse,*
> *Where nae horse should be.*
>
> *'What's this now, goodwife?*
> *What's this I see?*
> *How came this horse here,*
> *Without the leave o me?'*
> *'A horse?' quo she.*
> *'Ay, a horse,' quo he.*
>
> *'Shame fa your cuckold face,*
> *Ill mat ye see!*
> *'Tis naething but a broad sow,*

My minnie sent to me.'
'A broad sow?' quo he.
'Ay, a sow,' quo shee.

'Far hae I ridden,
And farrer hae I gane,
But a sadle on a sow's back
I never saw nane.'

Lewis never did hear the following verses. They were far too risqué for the ears of a young Aboriginal boy. But the sound of his voice in his new dark and murky world offers some solace. He repeats the ditty over and over.

[A'isha]

A'isha looks up as the breeze carries with it the strange sound. At first, she believes it's the humming of her guiding spirits showing her the way. Then rhythmic words take over in a language she has never heard before. *Have my friendly spirits aroused those of the evil kind?* She wonders. But one word she recognises…*horse!*

Can this be the boy soldier calling me to follow? If it is, then how does he know that I am?

As the crunching ground underfoot changes from pebbles to hushed sand, the singing ahead becomes clearer. Without realising, A'isha begins to step in time to the distant rhythm and the fear of loneliness in the desert is no longer.

Chapter 11
THE SANDSTORM

[Lewis]

The long walk through the night continues at a slow pace. Underfoot the ground has changed to soft sand. Despite this, Spade is favouring his injured leg more than when they started. This soft sand that began as a friend has become their enemy. The difficulty getting a firm footing has accelerated fatigue in both Spade's and Lewis' legs. What Lewis is unaware of is the tiny grains penetrating the socks and compacting into Spade's damaged hoof.

On top of this, the breeze that Lewis trusted to guide him toward the coast has changed so much it has become irrelevant. In fact, if Lewis could see where the sun is awakening, he would realise they are heading in the opposite direction.

His singing continues for company and sanity. The Scottish ditty, though, did become tiresome after far too many repeats. He did go through songs of his mob, but after the Scottish ditty, they didn't have the same rhythm to walk to. So he delved into the few ballads the white drovers sang when they herded cattle. It seemed to cast a spell over the animals who appeared to walk in time to the tune. Exactly what was needed to keep both him and Spade on the move.

He never learnt all the verses, just those he understood, like *The Queensland Drover*.

> *There's a trade you all know well*
> *It's bringing cattle over*
> *On every track, to the Gulf and back*
> *Men know the Queensland Drover*
>
> *Pass the billy round, my boys*
> *Don't let the pintpot stand there*
> *For tonight we drink the health*
> *Of every overlander*
>
> *I come from the Northern plains*
> *Where the girls and grass are scanty*
> *Where the creeks run dry or ten foot high*
> *And its either drought or plenty*
>
> *Pass the billy round, my boys*
> *Don't let the pintpot stand there*
> *For tonight we drink the health*
> *Of every overlander*
>
> *There are men from every land*
> *From Spain and France and Flanders*
> *They're a well mixed pack, both white and black*
> *The Queensland overlanders*
>
> *Pass the billy round, my boys*
> *Don't let the pintpot stand there*
> *For tonight we drink the health*
> *Of every overlander*

He sings this and other ballads over and over to brighten the oppressive darkness. But there's one ballad he sings only once, *The Dying Stockman*.

> *A strapping young stockman lay dying*
> *His saddle supporting his head*
> *His two mates around him were crying*
> *As he rose on his pillow and said*
>
> *Wrap me up with my stockwhip and blanket*
> *And bury me deep down below*
> *Where the dingoes and crows can't molest me*
> *In the shade where the coolibahs grow*
>
> *Oh had I the flight of the bronzewing*
> *Far over the plains would I fly*
> *Straight to the land of my childhood*
> *And there I would lay down and die*
>
> *Then cut down a couple of saplings*
> *Place one at my head and my toe*
> *Carve on them cross stockwhip and saddle*
> *To show there's a stockman below*

Though not sung again, the words echo in his head. The thought of dying here in this foreign land, where his body will lie on the sand for the scavengers, was becoming too real.

He reverts to singing the Scottish ditty just as the breeze becomes stronger. The hand that reassuringly lay on Spade's back is now used to hold his hat in place. The strengthening wind forces Lewis to lean into its intensity to keep momentum. Sand now peppers his face. Even with his eyes tightly closed, the grains find their way under the lids and cling to the crust of dried tears. He pulls the brim of his hat down to help shield his face. But what of Spade? Unlike camels with nostrils that can close, long eyelashes that help deflect most of the sand and a third eyelid that can wipe away any that manage to get in, horses don't have these features.

This is not the first sandstorms Lewis has experienced here in the Arabian deserts. He's also experienced many willy-willies and dust storms in the outback of Australia. But being blind and having no idea where they are or where they're heading is a different and challenging dilemma. For the first time in his life, Lewis feels lost.

[A'isha]

A'isha is also struggling. Obstacles continue to build and impede her progress. Lack of sleep has blurred her concentration, bringing on bouts of hallucination. Flashes of faces, bloodied and bruised, rush towards her. Some are laughing. Some are crying. Headless soldiers in varying uniforms are marching beside her in step and in time with the distant songs. Falcons fly overhead in ever-tightening circles creating a whirlwind of stinging scorpions. The hallucinations then become a reality. The whirlwind is the building sandstorm. The stinging is the sand on her face. The hem of her thobe, pulled up to carry her gathered food, expose her bare legs to the biting earth.

Her headscarf is covering her face with only a slit to see through. She tries to quicken her pace as the sound of the soldier's singing fades into the increasing roar of the wind. Soon the wind will erase the tracks she follows. The cloud of upheaved sand ahead glows orange as it filters the rising sun. The desert floor will be swept and a new layer of sand from somewhere distant will change the landscape.

Is it true that self-sacrifice can tame the evil desert spirits? It has been said to me so true it must be. I call on my beautiful patience and the Djinn powers that I now possess to abandon me in the hope it will give me strength and ease this biting wind.

A'isha lowers her head and struggles to make headway against the wind. The stinging grains of sand and dust begin to consume her. Each step becomes harder to take. Her thobe billows in the wind like the sail of a boat, doubling the energy needed to battle against the onslaught. Like most battles against nature, nature triumphs. All her remaining strength wanes. Her stubborn determination is sand-blasted away. She slumps to her knees, curls up into a ball and clasps the talisman around her neck. Within moments the colour of the earth covers her.

Oh mighty Allah, is it your will to bury me here? Am I never to return to my people? Will this be my eternal bed, to be unmarked and forgotten? If this is your will, oh mighty Allah, I succumb to your wishes…but with respectful regret.

[Lewis]

Lewis has an arm wrapped around Spade's head. His hand attempts to cover his horse's eyes from the invading sand. He calls on the spirit of the wind for forgiveness for any misgivings. Such was his mother's warning. *If he be bad fella, a spirit will show itself as the dust devil and take him into its whirlwind as punishment.* The chance such a spirit languishes in this foreign land is looking like a regretful possibility.

Without warning, Spade comes to an abrupt halt.

Lewis fears that if they stop it could be the end of them. He reasons that if they stop, they will endure the full depth of the storm for much longer. But if they continue, they will reach the end quicker. He walks ahead in a blind attempt to lead the way, only to collide with something solid. He runs a hand over the surface and feels stonework. A wall! The top has crumbled to chest height, enough, though, to shelter against the wind. He pulls on Spade's neck to get him to lie down. Together they huddle up against the wall as the rush of wind and sand roar overhead. Here they'll shelter and rest until it passes. But rest will not come easy. He can already feel the temperature rise as a new day looms. Soon the wind will subside. In its place will come searing heat. Will this wall offer enough shade? Is there more to this wall? Is there a building? Are there other people sheltering from the sandstorm? He stands in an attempt at calling out, but the howling wind blows his voice back at him. He will try again after the storm has passed.

Waiting out the storm lulls Lewis into a dream state. The need for rest is overpowering. His darkened world offers no diversion.

*

The storm has passed, and Lewis wakes to something

crawling over his face. Creepy-crawlies never usually worry him, but unable to see what it is, makes him swat around until he lands a blow on Spade. Spade reacts with a shake of the head, dislodging collected sand. Lewis removes his hat and shakes his red-tinged hair. He runs a hand over his face and feels the sandy crust around his eyes. Grains of sand have found their way under his eyelids and need to be washed out. The same must also apply to Spade. He removes the bridle, brushes off the sand that had collected under the leather, uncaps his water bottle and flushes the sand from his horse's eyes before his own. The water soothes. The residual pain he feels is the result of scratches to the eye's surface.

He places a hand on the top of the wall to help him stand. He feels the heat coming from the stone. A slight breeze on his face is also warm. The sun has risen. Light is reflecting off the sand and making him squint. Is his sight returning? He looks down at Spade. Everything is still darkish, veneered and blurred, but he can make out the bulky shape, his mane, his twitching ears and friendly face. As if in celebration, Lewis pours a little water into his hat for Spade to drink then a sip for himself.

Having even the slightest sight back lifts his spirits. He pulls the brim of his hat well down and takes his first look at where they've ended up.

The brim of his hat is shading his eyes from the sun, but the glare coming up from the sand is still painful. He covers his eyes with one hand and slowly spreads two fingers, masking most of the glare. This allows him to focus as much as he can on the finger-framed panorama.

There are no other buildings and no other people.

The crumbling wall is all that remains of a temple or dried-up well.

He looks down at Spade still slumped up against crumbling stones. *Was it luck or was it you, Spade, who led me here?* He chooses to believe the latter. But, while the wall was a welcome barrier against the raging wind and sand, it will not shade them much longer from the rising sun.

Turning his back to it, he peers through his spread fingers. There's a slight improvement in what he can see. But what he sees is not at all encouraging. The retreating sand storm is hugging the ground in the distance. Lewis blinks to help focus. He can just make out the tip of the hill they had left peaking above the dust cloud. He turns to look in the direction deemed north by the sun rising at his back. There is nothing to see but increasing heat haze. No floating hill or trees. Nothing but an open expanse of flat sand.

He looks back to the hill that offered them water and sanctuary from the heat. Going back is an option. But it will mean walking the whole day in the heat with no water. Considering the condition they're in now, the chances of making it is slim. He lowers his eyes to think. What other option is there? Maybe now that he has some sight, it could be possible. From where he stands he traces the ground back to the hill. Picturing in his mind the challenges a day's walk under hot sun will throw up at them.

Suddenly, the sense he felt during the night that someone was following returns. He ignored it as a slight bump in the sand as he traced his steps back to the hill.

He blinks and shakes his head hoping to defog his sight further. Now it's screaming out to him…no…for him!

He orders Spade to stay, grabs the water bottle and runs out into the desert

The only thing showing under the covering of red earth is strands of a brown headscarf. Lewis immediately scoops away the sand to uncover the girl rolled up into a tight ball. The only flesh showing is a hand holding the scarf over her head and clenching a talisman. He continues digging to reveal her other hand clinging tightly to her bundled up tunic beneath her. He feels for a pulse. It's faint. He folds back her headscarf. For the first time he lays his bleary eyes on the face of the Bedouin girl who stole his horse. He lifts her head to feed her a little of the remaining water. It dribbles from her clenched mouth creating rivulets through the caked sand on her chin. Her lips relax to the kiss of water, allowing some to enter.

"What you doing, silly girl fella? You bloody stubborn one, that for sure."

A'isha partly opens her eyes and blinks away some sand. Weakness can't keep them open.

"No use you sitting here praying, hey?"

He tries to help her to her feet by pulling on the arm wrapped around her waist. She wrenches it away from his grasp and tightens her hold on her bundle.

"What you got there girl? You little fella in your belly, hey?"

There's no reply, only the slump of her head.

"You better come with us then, hey? Could be we need each other."

Chapter 12
FROM OUT OF THE HEAT HAZE

[A'isha & Lewis]

A'isha is struggling with her emotions after her rescue from a premature burial. To be rescued by the boy soldier is an embarrassment that makes a show of appreciation difficult. With no words to call on, the offering of her lean harvest will have to do.

Hunger needs stemming and energy restored, no matter how small the pickings. Lewis is more than glad to accept. A'isha watches as he fumbles and struggles to identify what she had gathered. The realisation that he could see anything at all is a great relief to A'isha. It is a sign of further recovery. But his poor eyesight requires her help in separating the items.

Spade gets the plants and roots. Lewis discards the thorny plants, fearing they would do more damage than good. He places the mixed bag of insects, spiders and other creatures on the hot stones on top of the wall. The cooking will help remove any possible toxins, Lewis tries to explain. He chooses not to add that it will also make them a little more palatable in case it offends her.

Removing the skin from the snake with his teeth is something Lewis has done many times, so bad eyesight is not a handicap. It too goes on the wall.

The insects are eaten first to give the snake more

time to bake through. A'isha declines the white meat of the snake, thinking it may still carry the spell she had cast.

With the improvised feast over, the three are confined to the diminishing shade cast by the wall. A'isha is uncomfortable at the closeness of being tightly sandwiched between Lewis and his horse. Made worse when Lewis removes his shirt and holds it over their heads to add more shade.

If I ever find my family, they will instantly cast me out. I will be banished forever for having this foreign soldier's naked body against mine. The sweat of his armpit smells like the pungent ooze from the back of a male camel's neck.

While Lewis silently considers the next move, A'isha becomes lost in another confused uncertainty.

There is a strangeness I am feeling. Never have I rested so close to a male before. I wonder what he thinks of my odour. I feel ashamed in my unclean state. What has he seen of me when he removed me from my grave and carried me to this wall? My mind was unaware then, or maybe I slept. Did he seek to see more of my body? I have heard of soldiers and their lustful ways.

She takes a suspicious glance at Lewis and his naked dark torso streaked with sweat.

Now he shows off his body after casting eyes over mine. He has a distant look in his eyes. Is it a look of lustful satisfaction? I'm sure he went further than a look. My body is telling me it is so. His heathen hands have soiled my naked flesh.

With that thought in her mind, and despite her frailty, she leaps up, startling Spade and Lewis, and slaps him across his face. Her slurred grunts, groans and waving of hands in her muted effort to tell of her disgust and shame only add to Lewis' bewilderment.

"What you do that for, girl?" he says. "I think you gone bloody mad in the heat."

A'isha continues to utter soundless words. Frustration shows in her eyes as they begin to fill with tears.

Lewis reaches out for her. "You better sit back down, girl, or you get madder standing there in that sun."

I have lived all my life unable to speak. It was the will of Allah that I have no voice and so it to be natural. But I have never felt what I am feeling now. What has this boy soldier done to bring me to these tears? Can he not hear I am without voice?

She backs away with frustrated arm gestures. The patting of her mouth expresses her emotions while her distressing groans reach into the heart of Lewis.

"Why you not say you no can talk?" The insanity of the question brings a half smile to his face. "That pretty silly thing to say, hey?"

Lewis reaches for her again, but her gesturing has stopped. Her attention focusses elsewhere. Her face tightens, and she wipes away her tears. Lewis stands and turns to see what's caught her eye. The persistent remnants of the venom's blinding effect limits his sight to only the glare of a shimmering distant heat haze. But A'isha can make out two blurred shapes and the distinctive swaying gait of a pair of camels. Their riders gradually take shape the closer they come.

Lewis squints against the glare. He sees nothing. A look at A'isha confirms that she has. Her stare is intense.

He looks back into the blur of the desert and back again to try and read her response. Her silent stare provides no answer.

The white loosely wrapped Keffiyehs worn by both approaching Arabs hide all but their eyes. Their thobes, caught by the hot breeze, billow behind them. Each sits straight-backed with their left leg hooked around the front pommel of the camel's saddle. A'isha takes note of the saddles adornments. The thick, brightly coloured tassels that hang and sway in rhythm to the camel's stride will tell her a lot.

"What?" asks Lewis, still struggling to see.

A'isha raises a hand indicating he be silent as they approach the other side of the wall.

They're now within Lewis' struggling sight, but the sun reflecting off the white of their clothes blurs out any detail. That soon changes when they turn towards the wall with the sun at their backs. Their faces remain hidden, but their weapons are threateningly displayed. The taller of the two has a large curved sheathed dagger prominently tucked in his belt alongside a flintlock pistol. The other rider's dagger is at his side to allow for an ammunition belt full of cartridges to be slung over one shoulder and across his chest. A rather old Berthier carbine hangs from his other shoulder.

The relationship between the Australians and the Arabs during the Ottoman war was not always friendly. There was a high degree of mistrust from both sides. Some sided with the Turks, some didn't, and, even though the war was officially over, there was still pockets of resistance.

Instinct has Lewis reaching for his carbine, but it lies unattended back at the camp. Being partially in uniform with his shirt dangling by his side, all sorts of consequences spin through his head. They could shoot him and leave him to rot in the desert, and no one would be the wiser. Or, if they turn out to be friendly, they could turn him over to an Australian or British force. That would mean prison for desertion and no more Spade. He accepts fate is in their hands, drops his shirt and raises his arms in surrender.

There's an eerie silence as the Arabs contemplate what to do with a half-naked man and a Bedouin girl on the far side of a tumbled down wall. Unseen and unheard by the Arabs, there's a shuffle of hooves in the sand.

Lewis whispers out the side of his mouth. "Stay low Spade."

Spade interprets this as 'say hello, Spade'. The command Lewis used when they performed rodeo tricks together. He scrambles to his feet forcing the camels to gurgle and retreat a few step back at the unexpected sight of a horse. The riders quickly gain control of their camels and a few words in Arabic pass between them. Their headscarves are covering all but their eyes, revealing a dark brooding expression from one of them. He swings his carbine off his shoulder and aims it at Lewis. The other kicks his camel into a slow, reluctant stride around the crumbling wall and gestures to Lewis to pass him the rope now tied around Spade's neck. Rather than handing it over, Lewis grabs it and pulls Spade closer to him. The sound coming from the other side of the wall of a cartridge feeding into a gun chamber is all too familiar to Lewis.

The Arab again beckons for the rope. Lewis takes a moment to weigh up the situation. The dagger in his belt is less ornate than others seen during his time in Arabia. The sheath is leather covering carved wood with little silver trimming. The pistol in his belt is a flintlock musket serviceable more for protection rather than as a threat. But the one pointing a deadlier carbine at him is almost willing Lewis to give him any excuse to shoot. With no other sensible choice, Lewis reluctantly hands over the rope.

From his height atop the camel, the Arab looks over his find of a horse, a girl and a soldier. He kicks off Lewis' hat to study his face. The plumed hat is familiar to the Arabs as those worn by the Australian Light Horse, but all he has come across have been white men. This boy has brown skin like an Arab, despite the rarity of red in his hair. He gives Lewis a slow look up and down. His pants, belt, leggings and boots are army issue, as is the shirt now lying on the ground. After taking a moment to study Lewis' naked torso, he turns to A'isha with a disapproving shake of the head. With a pull on the neck rope, he kicks his camel into action. Spade digs in and refuses to move. The Arab yanks on the rope, not once but many times against Spade's stubbornness. A conversation between the two erupts into what Lewis assumes is an argument. The one holding the rifle calls to A'isha. As expected, she does not reply, and to Lewis' surprise, nor does she appear delighted to see her own kind.

A'isha is spoken to again, but silence is forever her response. He bends down and forcefully turns her head towards him. He searches her eyes before pushing back her headscarf. He ignores the bruising and scab of her head wound to study the tattoo on her forehead. He looks back at his companion while turning A'isha's face to show off her marking. After some words, they nod in agreement. The one holding the rifle waves it in the direction he wants A'isha and Lewis to move.

The moment I saw the two, a terrible fear swept over me. They are not of my clan and the colours of the braided tassels hanging from the camel bags are uncommon to me. This, I assume, means they have been displaced by the war and distant from their region. I feel they are Bedouin, but many a war is fought between clans…and we goat herders are looked down on from the height of their superior camels.

By the laws of the desert, they will not harm me as I am a girl, but I fear for the boy soldier. He could still be seen as the enemy as I saw him. I cannot defend him as I cannot speak. Nor would they listen.

I could be of value as a trade if they know of my tribe. If not, I would still be worth a female camel or two as marriage fodder. Though, now they have looked upon the sign on my forehead, my value as a mute may not be as high. I can only obey their command and follow and hope the boy soldier will do the same without complaint.

As soon as they start to move, the one leading Spade notices his faltering step. He dismounts from his camel by using the top of the fallen wall as a step. He bends back the favoured leg and checks the hoof. The improvised padding gets careful attention. He glances up at Lewis with a hint of approval. This helps to ease the fear Lewis has of their treatment towards Spade. He knows the

Arabs and Bedouin have a high regard for such a horse. But while they may look after him, that could turn out to be a big problem.

To protect their find of a valuable horse, it is decided the horse will carry no weight. The girl will ride with the one holding the rifle. As the horse shows reluctance to move without its master, the worthless soldier can walk by its side.

Half covered with sand, Spade's bridle is left lying against the crumbling wall.

Chapter 13
THE BEDOUIN CAMP

An hour has passed since leaving the wall and the hot sand is burning Lewis' feet through the heated soles of his boots. His eyes are permanently closed to block out the painful glare of the midday sun. One hand has a tight grip on the rope linking Spade to the camel ahead. The further they go the more the heat begins to play tricks with his mind. Ambient sounds start to scream out for individual attention. The soft plod of the camel's webbed feet on the sand challenge the crunch and grind of a horse's hooves. The grumble and grinding teeth of the camels broadcast their annoyance at having a horse for company.

But the sounds in his head are the loudest. The sounds of his past. The singing at his mob's corroboree. The crack of a drover's whip. The whistles and mooing of a cattle drive. The piercing screeches of pink-crested Galahs and the tapping of a billy to settle the tea. Sounds he will never hear again nor sight their making. They all come together in his homesick mind. They are his songs of Dreamtime. Using throat and nose breathing, the sound of a didgeridoo penetrates the still, hot air.

The Camels stutter. The Arabs spin their heads around with hands on weapons. A'isha continues to look worried, but the sound is not unfamiliar. Spade nods his head in recognition and understanding.

The further they travel, the blistering heat and incessant sun are taking their toll on Lewis. His mind begins to wander, as do his feet. He struggles to keep up the pace as well as maintaining a hold on the rope. Spade endeavours to slow down the leading camel by jerking his head back and pulling on the rope tied to its saddle. This ploy is short-lived when the frustrated Arab whips his camel back to speed. If Lewis did collapse, there is no doubt he would be left to cook on the hot sand. On the following camel, A'isha sits captive in the arms of the carbine-carrying Arab. She can only watch, tensing up with each faltering step the boy soldier takes.

*

Another hour in the heat of Hades and they finally come in sight of their destination. Any further and Lewis would not be with them.

Barely visible against a shallow rocky backdrop, the camp consists of one long, low-slung tent of woven goat hair. A'isha looks around for other tents. But there are none. A mix of emotions overwhelms her, for a single tent is only big enough for a family and not a clan. The closer they get her self-interest stirs. She examines every detail, hoping to find some answers. From where have they travelled? Would they know of my family? To her, their tent looks makeshift. Not purposefully transient as most nomadic Bedouin would have it. A sign of a rapid departure from their camp, with bits and pieces collected along the way added to their tent. Something that is not uncommon since the war began. Her family was under such a threat at one stage.

The sun is mercifully beginning its descent, and the rocky ridge will soon cast its shadow over the tent. One side of the tent is folded back, showing three divisions. Each is separated by hanging carpets of woven patterns in subdued colours. A rather time-worn blanket has been slung over one of the guide ropes to isolate the cooking area. Inside, a curl of smoke rises from a fire heating a round metal plate and a well used copper coffee pot. An old woman sits cross-legged on a small carpet beside the fire mixing dough. From her mouth hangs a silver and cane pipe the length of her arm. The glowing tobacco-filled bowl at the end rests on one knee. She looks up as the group, including two strangers, approaches. Immediately, she takes the pipe from her mouth and pulls her scarf across her tattooed face. A loose layered indigo-dyed thobe covers her body leaving only her eyes and hands visible. Around her neck hangs a silver talisman and a large ornate silver necklace weighed down by rows of coins.

Her expectation of seeing the men bringing back the evening meal is dashed. Disappointed, she returns to preparing her flatbread. A horse, maybe, but a girl and a struggling soldier were not what she expected, or wants.

A young boy runs out from behind the draped blanket on hearing their arrival. He brakes to a halt, surprised at seeing more than he expected. The two camels thump down onto their haunches and the men dismount. One takes the girl down while the other unties Spade's neck rope from the saddle. He hands the rope to the boy and orders him to take the horse behind the tent and tie him to one of the tent posts.

Spade is led away, leaving nothing to support Lewis. He struggles to stay on his feet due to exhaustion, dehydration and heat stroke. His vision is once again blurred. His head is throbbing and he dry-retches from nausea and stress. Groping for support, he staggers towards the central section of the tent just as an old man emerges. Their eyes meet for only an instant as Lewis grabs the tent pole and collapses at the old man's sandalled feet.

He looks down to where Lewis lies and follows with a questioning glance to the two men who brought him. His leathery face is deeply etched, giving him a look of suspicious intelligence. He has a grey stubble of a beard, coffee-stained and as coarse as the hairs on a desert hedgehog's back. He wears a plain white Keffiyeh topped by a dark woven band of camel hair. His long dark grey thobe, buttoned at the neck, drapes to the ground.

The two young men compete in talking over each other as they attempt to explain their unexpected delivery. One points to the fallen Lewis and the other points to A'isha left standing beside the sitting camels. The old man glances at her for only a second showing little interest. Having heard all he wants to hear, the old man puts a halt to the ongoing chatter with a raised hand. He waits to be sure he has their full attention then pats the tent post which Lewis lies caressing. He gives an order that seems to anger the shorter and younger of the two. He starts to protest. It's brief. The look from the old man at questioning his order is decisive. After a reluctant bow, he helps the other drag Lewis into the tent.

A'isha has seen enough. She looks down at the camels and steps back with a look of distaste.

All the way here my eyes did not leave the boy soldier. I once feared and loathed him. Now I'm confused with feelings I do not understand. My 'evil eye' is the cause of his pain. I saved him from blindness. He saved me from a desert grave. But what dangers he will now face…I know not.

I am pleased to see a familiar tent and the smell of coffee heating. I am pleased for the boy soldier to at last have a chance to rest. I watched him try to vomit. I watched his legs bend. I wanted to help him then stopped as he reached for the tent post just as the old man appeared. He is the head of the family, I'm sure. Seeing what the soldier holds on to, I know he will not go against desert courtesy.

The young boy returns from tying up Spade with an order from the old woman to bring the girl to her. He does so with a hint of a smile to A'isha and a soft touch on her arm as he leads her to sit beside old woman. She looks around and feels a degree of comfort in the surroundings. The patterned camel hair rug she sits on is threadbare and faded. The familiar layout of the cooking area and the tea and coffee utensils stir sad memories of her lost family. For the moment it's the best she could have wished for. She'll be a guest, fed and protected. In her heart, she believes it will be the same for the boy soldier. For according to Bedouin custom, the moment he held onto the main tent post he became a protected guest who'll receive shelter, liquid and food. In the three days it takes for the first meal to pass through his body, the obligation to protect him will end. This day he will receive tea or coffee for his thirst. Coffee for good cheer on the second day, and on the third day a coffee to get rid of him. How and by what means is the unknown.

With a shudder down her spine, a strange feeling comes over A'isha. She looks back to the old women. She has loosened her scarf revealing a face aged, hardened and covered in tattoos. Her eyes are staring at her with deep suspicion. The hairs on A'isha's arms and the back of her neck become erect. The tattoos are not just adornments from a past era, but patterns on the skin to deter evil and protect against the powers of the Djinn.

Meanwhile, Lewis has been dragged inside the tent and lies on a carpet covering the ground. The movement has stirred his mind, but his body remains limp and weak. There's a not-so-gentle slap to the side of his face with little response. A more robust slap follows, then another until his eyelids flicker. His lips move as the nauseous cloud rattles his confused head. Another slap opens his eyes further. More out of annoyance. His vision clears enough to make out the perpetrator. The carbine carrier seems to have taken a dislike to Lewis. He's about to make another strike when the old man intervenes. He's told to prop the soldier up against some cushions. Lewis is hoisted up so his limp body can take in some water.

He gulps the water too fast and a bubble gets stuck in his gullet. A cough followed by a loud burp loosens it and allows more water to get through. The realisation that he is still alive surprises him. The coolness inside the tent and lack of sun glare welcomes him back to the living. The dim light eases the strain on his eyes, allowing him to focus on his surroundings. Carpets cover most of the ground with a scattering of cushions of varying sizes and patterns. Curtains of woven goat hair partition the room. At his back is the rear wall of the tent. Facing him is the open front framing the panorama of the desert. The same desert that almost claimed him for eternity. One more look around the tent to confirm his survival is all he can manage before fading back to unconsciousness.

*

It's night by the time Lewis wakes. The open sides of the tent are now closed to keep out the cooling night air. The flickering glow from a small fire set in a square of swept earth fills the tent and highlights the faces staring back at him. The two who brought him to their camp sit at each side. The one with the carbine has it resting across his knees pointing at Lewis. Sitting opposite, on the other side of the fire, is a boy of uncertain age due to his undeveloped growth. He is frail, skinny with small shoulders and an elongated head. His uncovered hair is short and rather crudely cut. His ears sit at right angles to his scalp. His Thobe hangs frayed and dirty. A single strand of braided camel hair circles his neck. Attached is a small scarab of tarnished silver which he grasps in one hand. Beside him, on the plumpest cushions, resting on one elbow and one leg cocked, is the old man. He is devoid of any adornments or jewellery as is the custom of a clan leader.

A tray with an elegantly shaped brass teapot and five thick, squat glasses rest beside the fire. The old man has patiently waited for this moment. He leans forward to pour tea into the glasses. One, he hands to Lewis, who accepts with shaking hands and waits for the others to take up theirs. The tea is hot and ultra sweet. He feels his stomach contract as if to dry retch again but manages to control himself. The second sip is easier to take. Ensuring there will be no problem in accepting the customary three glasses.

His mind begins to clear and thoughts of Spade enter. He senses his closeness. In fact, Spade is directly behind him, separated only be the thin wall of the tent. Being of prized Arabian stock, Lewis hopes they will respect and look after him. But being of value could mean they'll more than likely sell him. That is something Lewis will not allow to happen.

Further thoughts of Spade are cut short when the old woman appears carrying a large platter of food. Following her is A'isha with a pot of coffee and more glasses. The two women gather up the teapot and empty glasses and leave without a word or a glance at any of the men.

Only once before had Lewis sat in a Bedouin tent and shared a meal and coffee. He escorted two officers as they visited a Bedouin camp to question their allegiance to the Turks. Officially, his role was to protect the officers. But unofficially, he was there because of his dark skin. The thinking being the Bedouin might consider he is of Arab descent. One of the Bedouin spoke some English and interpreted. Though Lewis spoke no Arabic, they would not know that. He would sit quietly with a look of understanding. It was hoped this would be enough for the interpretation to be honest. All this was a little beyond Lewis' understanding. But the one thing that stuck in his mind was his introduction to the pungent coffee. Thick, black, extra sweet and with a quarter inch of sludge on the bottom. Lewis did have a sweet tooth for honey ants and developed a liking for sweet dates, but the coffee was beyond sweet. So as not to offend the hosts, he drank the coffee offered. A sharp poke in the ribs from an officer's baton stemmed the urge to throw up until the meeting was over.

With the sickly smell of coffee once again invading his nostrils, he feels his stomach turn. Knowing he stopped himself from vomiting once before, out of courtesy to his hosts, he can do it again. There are no words spoken. Only some gestures of encouragement from the old man for Lewis to eat and drink. A sign, if only from him, that Lewis is a guest in his tent.

The food is more than welcome, though well short of the feast that could have been offered had Lewis been a wealthy Sheikh. Rice enhanced with herbs, dates, yoghurt, flat bread and some sun-dried locusts. These gave Lewis a nostalgic taste of the outback. The addition of cardamon made the coffee easier to drink.

With the meal over, a conversation can start. Lewis, knowing just a handful of Arabic words, can only listen. But there is little doubt they will discuss his presence.

Lewis leans back, feeling some strength returning, and studies his hosts. To his left is the one who continues to aim his carbine at him. As far as Arabs or Bedouin go, Lewis finds him rather good looking. That is, if it wasn't for the mix of anger, envy and suspicion in his dark and rather wide eyes. His skin is smoother, and if he were not of brown skin, he would almost pass as a white man. His dress indicates a rebellious nature. His turban is too loose, and his unbuttoned Thobe looks a size too big, suggesting it may be a hand-me-down. He has a silver and coin necklace against his bare chest. His belt is less ornate, and his dagger is pushed to the side as if he is embarrassed to show it. Unlike others Lewis has come across who love flaunting their daggers. The one thing he does enjoy flaunting is his ammunition belt and rifle. Lewis wonders how well he can use it, or even if he has used it.

Lewis is unsure why this man has so much hatred for him. Is it being a foreign soldier, or is it that he is Aboriginal? Whatever it is, he does not feel at all comfortable with this man.

On his right, sitting cross-legged, is the one on the lead camel. His uncovered face appears older and not as threatening. His skin is darker, and he has what looks like the start of an immature beard. His clothes are more layered. His head scarf, while now loosened, shows more care in its application. His belt is a blend of embossed leather and silver links secured by a double looped silver buckle. Stuffed into his belt is the large, curved dagger with a less than impressive etched silver handle, yet still intimidating. The flintlock pistol has been removed from his belt to enable him to sit and rests on the ground beside him.

Lewis accepts he is sitting with a father and three sons, though the young boy shares nothing of his father's or brother's ruggedness.

The rapid prattle continues as if he was not in their space. But then he hears the older brother say, 'al hisan'. It's not him they're discussing, but 'the horse'. He was a foreign soldier of no consequence. But Spade was another matter. The thought of them discussing his horse was not unexpected. But when the two older brothers look to be arguing, it becomes a major worry.

I bet them fellas argue over who get my horse! Them better start thinking it'll not be that easy.

Lewis looks to the old man. He has settled into his cushions, appearing disinterested in the continuing debate. He gives a hint of a wave to the young boy. Bored with the antics of his older brothers, he jumps up to fulfil his father's request. He adds a small amount of tobacco to the top burner of the shisha pipe and lights it with an ember from the central pit.

Chapter 14
TERMS AND CONDITIONS

[A'isha]

I have washed and feel less unclean. The food offered was filling and familiar. But this old woman treats me as if I am cursed. She no longer looks upon my face, yet blows smoke from her pipe at me. Is it because I have only the one tattoo on my forehead that brands me as a mute? No! When she first looked into my eyes, I'm sure she saw the power I did not believe I had. It makes me wonder why she no trusts the many tattoos covering her face that are meant to protect her from evil spirits. A face hardened by the weather and lacking charity. Her downcast mouth has a callous on the lower lip from the constant pipe smoking. Her status as the wife of the Sheikh is evident by the amount of silver jewellery, bracelets and rings she wears.

She endlessly mutters through lips tightly clutching her pipe, but I feel it is to herself. I understand some of what she says, but she often drifts into whispered mumblings.

I now hear men talking beyond the curtain. It is not until they raise their voices that I can understand some of what they say. One word I can hear clearly has me nervous…'sawaj'…marriage!

What A'isha could not hear was the value they were placing on her.

The heat from the small fire is beginning to replace the lost heat of the day. The open side of the tent is now closed, and the flickering light from the fire dances shadows around the five men. The air is cloudy with smoke from the fire and the shisha pipe. The younger son sits disinterested in the smoking and conversation of his brothers. He prefers to concentrate on Lewis. The dark skin, like his own, is bewildering for someone who has only cast eyes on white-skinned soldiers. Adding to his belief that a spiritual energy lingers deep within this stranger is the red tinge in his hair.

Lewis senses the young boy's penetrating eyes gazing at him. He looks up. Their eyes meet, and an uncertain scrutiny of each other follows. Then, as fast as their eyes made contact, the connection breaks. Lewis looks away, leaving the young boy mesmerised by what was revealed. He chances a quick glance back to his father and brothers to see if they too had noticed. Their involved conversation over the gurgle of the pipe make it obvious they had not.

The verbal tone of the three men continues subdued, no louder than the bubbling water of the shisha pipe. But it's not long before the discourse between the two older brothers turns heated. Their father, the head of the family and Sheikh of a scattered clan, reclines deeper into his cushion looking on with wise observance.

Despite appearing disinterested in his older brother's argument, the young Qamrani bin Abdullah has listened to every word. His thin, stretched body hunches over crossed legs. His head is bowed in thought. After a moment, his dark, unblinking eyes look back to the soldier reclining opposite. If there was ever any hint of a threat from this man, it has gone. In fact, he saw something that bonded them together. This soldier from a far-off country is a nomad just like him. With guiding spirits just like him.

He turns to his father and asks to be excused.

The Sheikh waves his hand as if brushing away a fly and Qamrani gets up to leave.

"Qamrani," his father calls out before he has left the tent. "Take the soldier to the sleeping quarters."

Qamrani may no longer fear the foreigner, but he is yet to conquer his nervous shyness towards any stranger. He fumbles in his attempt at making Lewis understand he must move. His Arabic is not understood, and he's wary of any physical contact.

"You…you come," he squeezes out in broken English and a beckoning hand.

Lewis is surprised at hearing words he understands. He looks back at the older brothers and the father, wondering if they also speak English. If the older brothers do, then they certainly didn't want him to know when they met at the wall. Feeling it's not his place to enquire at this moment, he lifts himself up to follow Qamrani. The dividing curtain is pulled aside for Lewis to enter the sleeping quarters. Lewis hesitates before passing the boy. He lowers his head till it's almost touching the boy's. Qamrani's eye widen, and he takes a step back.

"This fella need a piss," whispers Lewis.

The startled Qamrani looks confused.

"Piss!" repeats Lewis pointing to his crutch. "Pssssss," he adds hoping Arabs pissing makes the same sound.

Qamrani's eyes relax with a smile of understanding. "Pssssss" he copies and adds it to his list of English words.

He's about to open the tent flap when one of the brothers calls out. "Qamrani, where are you going with him?"

It's the younger of the brothers. He uncrosses his legs and stands with his carbine aimed at Lewis.

"He want pissss", replies Qamrani in Arabic with a stretched out English 'piss'.

Whatever conversation that was going on around the fire stops. All eyes now focus on the boy and Lewis.

"Pssssss?" questions the brother. "What this psssss?" He looks back at his father and older brother in case they knew. They both shake their heads in ignorance.

"He want to urinate," explains the young Qamrani.

As all will need to empty their bladder before retiring for the night, he's given a nod.

"You go with him, Runmaiz," orders the father to his rifle-brandishing son.

"I can keep an eye on him, father," offers Qamrani.

"As you wish, Qamrani, but Runmaiz still goes with you."

A slight smirk lifts one corner of Runmaiz's mouth. Being alone with the soldier in the dark could lead to all sorts of accidents. He joins his younger brother and Lewis as they exit the tent. As soon as they're outside in the darkness with the tent flap closed, Runmaiz pushes in front of Qamrani and trips Lewis.

Lewis was expecting something, but not so soon, and he falls flat on his face. A heavy hand stops Qamrani from helping Lewis up.

"Let him crawl," says Runmaiz to the dismay of his young brother.

Lewis does not understand what's said and starts to get back on his feet. A sandalled foot stomps him back down. Intimidation is not new to Lewis. He grew up a black man in a white man's world back in Australia. While he may have retaliated back home, here there was too much at stake.

Qamrani attempts to push his older and stronger brother away from Lewis. "Runmaiz, stop, or I will tell our father how you treat his guest.'

This threat has some resonance and Runmaiz steps back. But he cannot help himself and points his rifle at Lewis while making a popping sound with his lips. "Take him to have his pssssss then. I will watch from here."

After relieving himself, Lewis is ushered into the sleeping quarters. Qamrani points to where he is to sleep before pulling the dividing curtain closed behind him.

Runmaiz's failure to deliver more harm to the soldier has left him angry. Not knowing what's said between his father and brother behind his back shows his insecurity. He attempts to reignite the argument they were having before he followed the soldier out. After some time and with no resolution forthcoming, the Sheikh loses patience.

He raises himself up from his reclining pose. Takes a

deep inhale of smoke from the pipe and releases a thick cloud towards his sons. It gets their attention, and with a hand raised he silences them.

"My sons," he says in a calm but stern tone. "I have listened to your argument. I have heard your disrespect for each other in which I am disappointed. You have a choice of two options. Each one of value yet you bicker over only one of those options."

His two sons glance down at the carpet they sit upon. To disappoint their father does not go well for either of them and their hope of succeeding him as head of the family.

"Both of you have arrived at an age," the Sheikh continues. "when you each should have a wife, the start of your own family, and, I may add, maturity."

Runmaiz bin Abdullah lifts his head to speak in his own defence. Once again he is silenced by the raised hand of his father.

"Because of this unexpected windfall, you have two choices. A young virgin to take as your own or to trade for a profit. Or, to own a proud Arabian horse, which, I confess, I have also cast a tempted eye over." He pauses to make sure the options had sunk in. "And what do I hear from you? Both claiming the horse for your self-image. A status symbol. If not for your arrogance, the horse would make a worthy offering for the hand of a daughter of a wealthy Sheikh. He would indeed see such an animal as a status symbol. You would then join our families together and prove yourself a worthy successor."

The pause allows Jumaa Ayed, the older of the two, a chance to speak.

"Sir, I beg your forgiveness," he says with a bow. "Of the two choices, I will accept what you deem suitable for me without question."

"I too!" snaps Runmaiz, not wanting his brother to get the glory of submission.

"Very well," agrees the Sheikh, taking another draw on the pipe and indicating they should both partake.

The brothers rush to take up their respective mouthpiece and share in a hit of apple-scented tobacco. Their clumsy haste exposes their eagerness to hear what fate their father will impose on them.

"What I offer you, I want you to think about with great care." He pauses with a look to each. "It will not be what you end up with, but how you go about achieving it. That will determine who I see fit to succeed me."

"A race!" calls out Runmaiz without hesitation. "He who rides the horse fastest over a set distance wins the horse."

"I will agree with that," responds Jumaa, confident he is a better rider.

"And what of the girl?" asks the old man. "Is she of no concern? Is it only the horse that retains your interest?" He takes another puff on the pipe under the nervous gaze of his sons. "Then I agree."

There is great relief felt by the two brothers at the prompt acceptance of their proposal.

The old man continues. "The day after next, he who rides the fastest wins the horse." He pauses as the two young men nod to each other at the challenge. "But," he adds with a sharpness to his tone. "The loser is to marry the girl."

"But father, she is marked a mute and of no worth," protests Runmaiz.

"We know not of her family or their status. It is only she who benefits from becoming one of us," adds Jumaa.

"That is my decision," says the Sheikh with a nod to the tent exit. His sons stand, accepting the finality of the discussion. "And remember," he adds. "I do have another son and heir."

[Lewis]

Lewis lowers himself onto the worn carpet of the men's sleeping quarters. Soft cushions surround him, but they are for the three sons to sleep on. The closed curtain separates the sleeping quarters from the muffled voices beyond.

The food has given him some energy, but he has still to make up for his lack of sleep. He lies back with his arms behind his head and tries to put all that has happened into perspective.

If things had gone as planned, he and Spade would have reached the coast by now and be well on their way to a new life. *If not for that bloody girl! She big trouble and the sooner I get Spade and ride off the better. Then she be outta my life forever.*

Lewis has no idea how long the Sheikh's hospitality will last. But one thing is for sure, if they do let him go, it will be without Spade. He'll make the most of whatever time he has to build up his energy and allow Spade's injured hoof to heal. Then they will escape.

It then dawns on him. He has not laid eyes on Spade since collapsing.

Him better be safe, fed and looked after! He threatens. *And where they got him?* He closes his eyes and frowns in deep concentration. It takes some time, but the strong connection between the two finally reaches through the wall of the tent. A murmur rumbles from the depth of Lewis' throat. A muffled snort is the immediate reply followed by the signature scraping at the sandy ground. If not for the woven back wall of the tent, Lewis could reach out and rub Spade's nose.

*

As morning approaches, darkness still hides much of the detail in the sleeping quarters. Lewis succumbed to his need for sleep. But it was short and restless due to the lingering anxiety over Spade. The urge to get up and check on Spade is impossible as he is sandwiched between the two older brothers. Their heavy breathing and snoring reminding him of his fellow soldiers back at camp. *What they think about right now?* He wonders. *Bet them fellas no think about me. Bet them fellas more worried about leaving their own horses right now.*

Outside the clouds part to reveal a third quarter moon. Through the air vent at the top of the tent, a thin line of moonlight catches the lingering smoke from the fire and shisha pipe. Lewis follows its ghostly beam down the partition that divides the living quarters. The colours and shapes of the woven pattern are incomplete in the glow. Lewis interprets them as Dreamtime spirits.

As the moon continues its slow sweep across the sky, so does its beam of light sweep across the tent interior until it falls on the face of the young Qamrani. He's awake, sitting up and staring back at Lewis. The whites of his eyes are pinpointed by the shaft of moonlight.

Chapter 15
A SENSORY TRIANGLE

The early morning sun is casting long shadows across the desert. The sand, once smoothed by the recent windstorm, now reveal the traffic of the night creatures. The zigzag slide of a cobra and the scuttling tread of a lizard divided by the trail of its tail. Delicate footprints of desert mice and the heavier marks left by a prowling fox.

The disturbed sand at the rear of the tent bears witness to the agitated movement of Spade during the night. Dejected, he rests his tender hoof on its tip. His head hangs in contact with the woven goat hair of the tent wall. The sense of closeness to his friend Lewis on the other side is little consolation to the lack of visual or physical connection.

The camels sit nearby in the fresh light of day and resume their scrutiny of this unwelcome intruder.

There's stirring inside the tent with the first crackle of tinder set to flame. The old woman, Faizah Yemena, has the morning meal of bread, yoghurt and coffee to prepare before the men of her family rise. Except for her youngest son, Qamrani. He has the task of gathering firewood and tending to the camels. This morning he will have help.

A'isha spent the night in the kitchen space with the suspicious and irate Faizah. Deprived of sleeping with her husband to guard over the girl has only added to her dislike towards her. The sense of a Djinn in the girl has the old woman weighed down with every talisman she owns. Her face is smeared with date seed oil to enhance the protective indigo tattoos. She abandoned the idea of securing A'isha's hands behind her back with a bracelet of clinking silver coins. It would have alerted everyone in the tent of her attempted escape, but the risk of spiritual reprisal was not worth it. Instead, tying a bracelet of clinking coins around her ankle would have to do. A'isha neither attempted an escape nor conjured up any spiritual revenge.

"Qamrani!" calls his mother as she fans the growing flames.

The young boy rises from his observance of the soldier and eases himself out of the men's sleeping quarters so as not to wake his brothers. He's well aware the soldier is already awake and is left staring at the back wall of the tent.

"Yes, mother," he replies on entering the kitchen area.

"Take the girl and gather more fuel for the fire," she demands. "And keep a watchful eye on her for she may try to steal a camel and flee."

"Yes, mother."

The young Qamrani is well aware of his low standing within the family pecking order. His physical impediment is a source of mockery from his brothers. They treat him as they would a lowly goat herder as opposed to their own self-esteem as camel-riding warriors. On top of all that, his mother treats him like a daughter, though loved and protected. The dismissiveness of his existence is seen differently by his father. The lack of manliness in someone he sired reflects poorly on him, but he is wise enough to see beyond the fragility. He sees intelligence and sensitivity that is lacking in his older sons. He also sees something else that is too deep for him to understand.

All this jibing mockery is of no great concern to Qamrani. He lives in his private world of perception. He prefers a daughter's chores anyway and finds the bravado attitude of his older brothers insensitive and banal. If they had their way, the horse soldier they plucked from the desert would not be worth living. The customary protection imposed on him by their father is seen only as a three-day reprieve. After that, his fate will be in their hands. But Qamrani has sensed something that even his father has not. The fate of the horse soldier may not lie in the hands of his brothers—or even the will of Allah.

[A'isha]

Having an alarm bracelet tied to her ankle overnight did not faze Aisha one bit. It never was her intention to flee…well, not at this very moment anyway. She is well aware the horse needed rest and for its injury to fully heal before attempting an escape. But what has fazed her is what she heard through the dividing wall of the tent that night.

If I am forced to marry either of the two sons I would rather take a knife and slit my own throat. My father's choice of a husband would be preferable. He may be old and not easy on the eye, but a wiser choice I'm sure.

Her thoughts are interrupted as Qamrani grabs her

arm and pulls her to her feet. The coins on her ankle bracelet erupt into a chiming chorus.

"Come girl. You must work to earn your welcome here." The abruptness of his tone betrays the acceptance of his disability. This girl is young, slender, a captive and offers a rare opportunity to show some manliness.

Aisha is surprised at the boy's change of attitude as she has only seen tenderness in his eyes. She searches for it again, but his eyes divert to the ground. She senses his embarrassment at being slightly shorter than her. But his grip on her arm exposes a hidden strength.

"Mother, can you remove the bracelet from her ankle? It will annoy the camels. I'll make sure she does not escape."

"She can do it herself," replies his mother as she lights up her pipe. "But do not trust her. She has evil in her, that one."

Qamrani's eyes flick in the direction where the soldier still reclines out of view. *Are they two of a kind?* He wonders. Rather than being worried, Qamrani feels a tinge of excitement.

After removing the bracelet, she is led to the rear of the tent. The five camels sitting on the ground give her a quick glance. They pause their masticating for an instant before returning to their vigilance of Spade.

A'isha snatches her arm from the boy's grasp on seeing the sad-looking Spade and starts toward him. Qamrani catches up and grabs her arm again. There's a struggle as A'isha tries to free herself once more.

"Is your concern for the horse or your freedom?" he asks.

Aisha looks back at him with an uncertain air and her lips part as if trying to form a word.

This time their eyes do meet. A'isha again sees the tenderness she had judged before. Then, unexpectedly, his expression changes. His eyes appear to focus on something flaring and far distant in A'isha's eyes. What she sees in his eyes is an undulating range of emotions. From initial fear to bewilderment, then to judgement and finally understanding. A faint smile of discovery washes over his face. He reaches out to take her arm once again. This time his grasp is gentle.

"Come, we need to gather fuel for the fire."

*

A'isha and Qamrani are returning with arms laden with sticks, dead grass and dried camel dung. A breeze captures a loose strand of A'isha's long hair. She stops to look towards Spade who is digging at the ground and hears a low murmur coming from inside the tent. A strange stillness descends over the area. The camels stop chewing, and their long-lashed eyelids slowly close. Spade turns his head toward A'isha and gives a slight nod. The murmur is the same she once heard coming from the boy soldier. She turns her concentration to the tent wall where beyond he must lie, then back at Spade. Their eyes meet for a moment before Spade turns to face the tent again. Three points of a sensory triangle are mysteriously connected.

The wind transforms into a gust that ruffles Spade's mane and A'isha's hair. The tent side flaps with a loud crack like a stock whip. Qamrani looks on in a silent trance. His tunic hangs straight and undisturbed by any wind as if cocooned in a bubble of still air. Entrance to their triangle has been denied him.

After an indefinable moment, the wind drops. The camels open their eyes and continue grinding their jaws as if nothing happened. Spade slowly lowers his head to rest against the tent wall again. His legs are straight and evenly spaced to support his weight and he appears to be falling asleep.

A'isha is not completely sure what has just happened, but she cannot ignore the residue it has left in her mind. A hint of a smile lightens her expression as she joins the unaware Qamrani in delivering their gathered fuel.

Chapter 16
NO WATER

The slap of the wind gust on the side of the tent has stirred the two brothers from their sleep. Lewis is already awake and sitting up, having mentally and spiritually connected with his horse. But the added connection to the Bedouin girl has left him wondering. His distant stare has the brothers searching to find the object of his interest. They will not see it, of course, being in Lewis' mind.

Runmaiz and Jumaa look at each other and shrug their shoulders and shake their heads at this crazy man. Their interest in the soldier is short-lived as preparing for the race fills their heads. They jump to their feet as sibling rivalry clicks in.

"Qamrani!" they call out in unison.

There's no reply.

"Qamrani! We need you, come here," adds Jumaa.

"Now!" yells Runmaiz in his aggressive manner.

The sound of dumped sticks precedes the patter of sandalled feet in the sand. Qamrani appears at the entrance to the sleeping quarters with a worried look. He glances at his brothers and then to Lewis who is looking back confused.

"Qamrani, stay here and watch over the soldier," instructs Jumaa.

"He is not to move from where he rests…understand!" Runmaiz adds in his usual attempt at dampening his older brother's dominance.

Qamrani nods his understanding while hiding his eagerness to spend every possible moment with the soldier.

After the two brothers leave, Lewis has an uneasy feeling that something is going on and it's better to have them in his sight than not.

Both Jumaa and Runmaiz are aware that much needs to be done before the following day's race. The day is new, and they're eager to get started. First, is to get acquainted with the horse after so much time riding camels. Moreover, camels with saddles. Unfortunately, what saddles they have are suited for humped animals, not for a straight-backed horse that is also missing its bridle and reins. That leads to the second problem that needs mastering—riding the horse bareback with only a neck rope to steer him.

Who rides first is also in the realm of the unknown. This decision is in the hands of their father and kept secret until just before the race. Therefore, the one who has the horse's trust will be in a more favourable position if he happens to ride last on a tired horse.

But their wish for an early start is delayed by a greater priority. One thing Faizah Yemena cannot tolerate is abuse of the time she puts in preparing meals for the men in her family, especially the first meal of the day. When it is ready to eat, so must they sit and eat.

"Where is Qamrani?' she asks.

"He's watching over the soldier," replies Jumaa.

"Then bring them both here. I will take food to your father so there is space for the stranger to sit. She can eat where she is," she adds with a disgruntled twitch of her head towards A'isha stacking firewood in a corner.

There's a restrained urgency to finish the meal first by Jumaa and Runmaiz. To not linger and savour her simple fare would enrage their mother.

Runmaiz pushes the restraint to its limit and no further. He jumps up wiping his mouth with the back of his right hand and rushes to the rear of the tent.

Jumaa gulps down the piece of flat bread he'd just torn off and dipped in yoghurt. Washing it down with coffee, he scrambles to his feet with a loud burp.

"Stay and keep these two here," he instructs Qamrani before rushing to catch up with his brother.

Lewis looks on, unsure of what's happening. Then fear and anguish washes over him on hearing Spade neighing and stomping the ground. He jumps up to see what's upsetting his horse as A'isha watches on, also showing concern. Qamrani places a hand on Lewis' shoulder in an attempt at stopping him. His hand is brushed aside only to have a heavier hand on Lewis' other shoulder forcing him back down. He looks up at the Sheikh's wife holding a heavy brass coffee pot in her other hand and primed to swipe.

"My horse! What them fellas doing to my horse?" Lewis calls out spinning his head back to Qamrani knowing he spoke some English.

A'isha has picked up a solid stick from the pile of firewood ready in case things got a bit messy. But peacemaker Qamrani sees her and shakes his head. She lowers the stick but keeps a firm hold on it.

Qamrani turns to Lewis. "Your horse will not be harmed, I assure you," he says with as much conviction as he can muster from his high-pitched immature voice.

Lewis searches the boy's eyes for a hint of truth. Not at all convinced, he looks up at Faizah Yemena. Her cold, stern look and a threatening coffee pot are enough to convince him to sit back down. He glances back at A'isha with the hope of some support. She lowers her eyes, conceding nothing can be done.

It has become painfully evident that both brothers have a challenge on their hands. Spade is already agitated and stressed. The camels tethered nearby aren't helping with their continual grunting and spitting.

Runmaiz, in his eagerness, is the first to approach Spade who backs away as far as the tethering rope will allow and pounds the ground with his front legs. Runmaiz grabs the rope and tries to pull the horse to him. Spade rears up with a mournful whinny, forcing Runmaiz to backtrack quickly. Without hesitation, the short-tempered Runmaiz decides to adopt an aggressive approach. He picks up a stick that has dropped from the gathered firewood. It's jagged with sharp protrusions where the side shoots have broken off. Runmaiz raises it with the intention of beating the horse into submission only to have Jumaa grab it from behind.

"No, young brother, you will only make the horse detest us. We need to gain the horse's trust."

Runmaiz snatches the stick back, aggrieved once again by his dominating older brother. "You are wrong,

Jumaa. Like the camels, that horse needs to be shown who its master is."

"No, you are the one who is wrong, Runmaiz," snaps Jumaa. "Your camel is the angriest. It bites and spits farther than any of the others. Now move away from the horse!"

Runmaiz stands firm for a moment in defiance and defence of his ego. But superiority is not to be challenged in their culture. He goes to throw the stick away in bitter defeat but hesitates, hides it behind his back and steps aside.

Unfortunately for Jumaa, the antagonising antics of Runmaiz has left Spade nervous and jittery. He tries to back away from the approaching Jumaa, but the rope is already tight. Such a restriction is threatening to Spade. He rears up showing his aggression. Jumaa tries to calm the horse with gentle words, but Arabic is not familiar to Spade and has no effect.

Meanwhile, the camels have become flustered and stressed by a rearing, stomping and bleating horse. They shuffle to stand and back off, but they too are constrained by tethered ropes. Adding to the developing mayhem, the two brothers now boisterously argue who is best to control Spade.

The tent shakes with Spade pulling on the rope tied to one of its posts. The camels have started their chorus of protest, adding to the yelling and commotion. All this is too much for Lewis. He again attempts to stand. This time he is stopped by the arrival of the Sheikh who has come to see what all the commotion is about.

With her husband now in control, Faizah adopts her

usual disinterest in what is obviously men's business. She gestures for A'isha to follow her out of the kitchen area and ignore what is none of their concern.

Qamrani is watching Lewis intently. He's intrigued by the pain and frustration showing on the soldier's face. He waits, expecting Lewis to bring into force some of the power he believes he has. But none is forthcoming. He gets to his feet as the racket beyond intensifies. Before leaving the tent, he glances back at Lewis with a look of confused disappointment.

"Stop," he calls out as he approaches his arguing brothers.

He is, of course, ignored and they continue to quarrel.

Qamrani stands his ground. "Neither of you will ride the horse unless his inflamed leg is tended to."

It takes a moment for his words to cut through the arguing. In their haste to win over the horse's trust, they have ignored its injured leg.

"Let the soldier tend his horse," calls Qamrani. "You will only make the injury worse and the race will be cancelled. Be aware, brothers, for a damaged horse will lose whatever value it has."

Runmaiz is ready to laugh at such a suggestion from his weakling brother, but Jumaa sees sense in it.

"Bring him here," he orders Qamrani while pulling Runmaiz back from the enraged animal.

As the young boy runs into the kitchen area, he's stopped by his father.

"What are you doing, Qamrani?" the old man asks. "I want whatever is happening out there to stop."

"Father, the horse will not allow Runmaiz or Jumaa

near him. He needs his leg treated, or he could go lame and become worthless except for a meal." Qamrani knew he was stretching the fact, and looks toward Lewis hoping he may have understood.

Lewis catches the eye of the Sheikh. "Sir, I don't know what's said, but me got pretty good idea what's…"

He's cut short by the Sheikh's raised hand and a look of dismay at being spoken to when not asked.

There's a thoughtful pause before the old man speaks again.

"Take him to the horse. But Qamrani," he lowers his voice to a whisper. "Make sure Runmaiz has his carbine with him. If the soldier tries to flee with the horse, tell him to shoot him."

Before Qamrani has a chance to lead Lewis out of the tent, his father beckons him closer.

"And Qamrani," he again whispers, but this time softer and closer to his ear. "The horse is not to be given water until after the race."

Qamrani is taken aback by this order as the race is not until the next day. But knowing not to question his father, he leads Lewis to the rear of the tent.

Lewis is shocked and angered at what he sees.

Spade is rearing up as far as the neck rope will allow, causing red abrasions to his neck. The older brothers are standing well back and out of kicking range but continuing to debate the issue. Despite the efforts of Jumaa to stop him, Runmaiz is again threatening Spade with the stick while yelling in anger.

"What you doing, you bloody crazy Arabs?" Lewis yells.

He rushes to his horse and gets between it and the two men. Runmaiz now turns his rage on Lewis. The blow from the stick to his back makes him grimace. But Lewis is happy to take it rather than his horse.

Spade responds instantly to the sight and sound of Lewis' voice. He stops rearing up but continues to dig at the sand with a shake of his head.

The touch of Lewis' hand on Spade's neck calms him down. Lewis feels the abrasions from the neck rope.

"Sorry, mate," Lewis whispers as he slides his arm over Spade's neck. "This is what I wanted to save you from. And this bloody dumb black fella has led you straight to it."

Behind Lewis the double metallic click and slide of a carbine bolt action can be heard. He lowers his head without turning around. He knows who'll be pointing a rifle at him, but chooses to ignore it.

"This horse needs water," he calls out in the calmest tone he can, despite his inner rage.

The two brothers do not understand what Lewis says. All they can do is look on with distrust as Qamrani comes to the side of Lewis and touches his arm for attention.

"No water," he says with a shake of his head.

In the heat of the moment, Lewis had forgotten the boy spoke English. But those two words immediately register.

"What you bloody mean, no water!" He looks back at the two older brothers. "This horse die for bloody sure if no water."

Jumaa and Runmaiz are equally confused when Qamrani passes on the instructions from their father.

"But he races tomorrow," questions Jumaa.

Runmaiz remains quiet. This new revelation could fall into his hands if he can persuade his father to let him ride first.

Lewis grabs Qamrani by the shoulder and gives him a firm shake.

"What's going on? You tell this fella. Hey!"

Again Qamrani feels an energy rip through him from the soldier's touch. He looks up into Lewis' dark, threatening eyes and sees a hint of fire in them. He grabs at the scarab pendant hanging from his neck and presses it to his lips and then to his forehead.

This is not the answer or response Lewis is after and he shakes the boy's shoulder again, this time with more force.

Jumaa and Runmaiz take a step forward in defence of their young brother. Spade rears up at their approach and at the same time giving out a loud deep-throated whinny.

Qamrani turns to his brothers with a shake of his head and a nod for them to step back.

Lewis is not interested at all in the older brothers. He just wants answers.

"You tell me, boy. You tell me what's going on."

"My English not good," reminds Qamrani still grasping his pendant.

"Mine bloody bad too," says Lewis with a hint of humour to allay any fear the boy may have toward him. "Just tell this fella what's happening with my horse."

"He race."

"Race!" Lewis cries out and looks around. "Race

against who…the camels?"

Qamrani gives him a cautious shake of the head.

"What then?"

"Time," mumbles Qamrani.

"Time? What you mean time?"

"He who ride the fastest."

Lewis needs to digest this before he continues.

"Them fellas?" He nods in the direction of Jumaa and Runmaiz. "Them fellas ride my horse?"

Runmaiz is not happy that they appear to be talking about him. "Qamrani, what is all this talk?" he calls out and gives his older brother a quick glance.

Qamrani ignores his brother and nods to Lewis.

"This bloody mad. Them fellas only know how to ride camels."

Qamrani shows his agreement with silence.

"How far then?" Lewis asks with a shake of his head. "How far they run?"

"Not far," Qamrani replies with some uncertainty.

Lewis can only shake his head in disbelief. "This horse cannot run on a sore leg. You tell them," he says waving a finger towards Runmaiz and Jumaa.

Runmaiz has run out of patience. He's had enough of not knowing what they're talking about and the delay in preparing the horse for him to ride. He steps forward with his carbine raised. "Little brother, stop wasting time and get him to hold the horse so I can ride him,"

Jumaa places a hand on the rifle and pushes it down to stop his brother going any further. "Qamrani, what is all this talk? What is the soldier saying?" he asks in a more measured tone.

Without looking back at his brothers, Qamrani answers. " He says the horse not fit to run on injured leg."

The fact that the soldier is beginning to control the situation is infuriating Runmaiz. "You tell this useless foreigner that if the horse is not fit to run it is worthless and fit only for the cooking pot."

Jumaa regrettably sees some reasoning in his brother's outburst. "Qamrani, make sure the soldier understands what your brother is saying."

Lewis is not interested nor understands what is said. "Listen! I don't care what you all are saying. No one rides this horse, right?"

"You fix horse," asserts Qamrani without adding the otherwise threat.

Lewis senses the boy is holding something back. He glances back at the older brothers. A lesson learnt during the past two years is that these people do not back down from anything without a threat. His life is worthless anyway, so the only thing they can threaten him with is the life of his horse. He turns to Spade and strokes his nose. Spade remains stressed.

"Then get water."

Qamrani takes a gulp of air and kisses his pendant.

"No water," he says without being too forceful. "No water till race done."

Lewis accepts the boy is only the messenger but can't help snapping back at him. "That bloody crazy, boy. If he don't end up bloody lame, having no water will kill him anyway. Why?"

"I no question my father. No water!"

Lewis looks around to see if the Sheikh is in sight.

He's not. If the order had come from the brothers he would fiercely argue against it. But coming direct from the father makes debating the issue hopeless. Lewis senses there must be some other reason for such a harsh order, considering the respect he would hold for a pure-bred Arab horse.

Defeated, he looks down at the quivering right foreleg of Spade. All he can do is lessen the damage and hope memory of the charge at Beersheba will carry him through—when he and the other horses charged after being without water for almost two days.

Chapter 17
PREPARING SPADE

[Lewis]

Repairs on the run are not uncommon in the Light Horse. Battles wait for no one and whatever the problem, it's either fixed, patched-up or replaced.

On this occasion replacement is out of the question and it will take far more than a day for Spade's damaged hoof to heal. That leaves patching him up. But with little to work with, the only help he can call on is from a small, slightly underdeveloped, shy, intense and nervous boy. But what demands can be asked of him that will be acceptable? Lewis needed to find out.

"What's your name?" he asks, in need of forming a friendlier relationship.

"Qamrani," the boy replies. Then, with a degree of uncertainty and fear that he is stepping into a realm of intimacy with a stranger, he asks. "Wha…what name do you have?"

Lewis has already turned his mind to his horse and automatically responds with, "Trooper Lewis Dun…" Then realises being a deserter means he is no longer a trooper. "Lewis! Just call me Lewis."

"Lewis," Qamrani whispers several times to himself to get used to the name.

Lewis turns his attention back to Spade and slides a

hand over his trembling foreleg then turns to Qamrani.

"Well, Qamrani, this fella can do with plenty help. You okay with that?"

It takes a moment for Qamrani to understand what Lewis has asked. He has a sly look back at his brothers. Would they object? The two have settled down in the shade of the tent discussing how their father will decide who will ride first. Runmaiz has his rifle resting across his knees pointing at Lewis.

"Um…yes…I…I…okay…Lewis," he replies, taking advantage of their distraction.

"You bloody good fella, Qamrani. Now…" He glances back at the brothers aware what he is about to ask for will test their reaction, "…if my horse not allowed water…he must have shade."

Expecting the boy to confer with his brothers, he's surprised by the immediate response.

"I will arrange."

Qamrani ignores a passing comment from Runmaiz and disappears into the tent. A short time later he returns with a couple of carpets that had lined the ground in the kitchen area.

Faizah Yemena had protested until Qamrani told her he had asked permission of his father. Which he did, but his father was resting and brushed him off with a reminder that no water be given to the horse. All Faizah could do was to shrug her shoulders, shake her head and puff heavily on her pipe at the strange goings on with the men. A carpet confiscated was one A'isha sat on while she ground wheat. She smiles to herself at the displeasure it gave the old woman.

With the help of Lewis, they attach a makeshift frame to the back side of the tent and the carpets are then slung over. The shade gives some relief from the heat of the sun. Now Lewis can concentrate on Spade's inflamed leg. It calls for something cold and wet wrapped around the leg, but when asked, anything to do with water is out of the question.

Despite the taboo on water, Spade is more relaxed having shade and his friend with him. Now it all goes down to care and whatever treatment is on hand.

First, removal of the shoe and packing from the damaged hoof is needed to clean and assess what can be done. If they were back at the camp, he'd have all the necessary equipment. But here in a small isolated Bedouin camp, he was unsure what was available. When he explained to Qamrani what he needed to remove the shoe and straighten the nails, it surprised Lewis what the boy came up with. Expecting something better than crumbling rocks, he was delighted when Qamrani produced a mallet used to hammer in the tent pegs, a flat stone of hard granite used for chopping up goat bones, and very large iron forceps. When asked what it was used for, Lewis cringed when told that besides turning hot embers in the fire, it was used to extract infected teeth. Mainly from camels, Qamrani calmly adds.

What Qamrani had come up with was good, but far from real farrier gear. This made removal of the shoe a problem. Each tug, tap, twist and levering caused some pain. When he reattached the thrown shoe back at the hill, Lewis found the crumbling rocks useless in bending over any nails that protruded. Also, without a file, he left them hoping the covering sock would cushion the points. Therefore, straightening the nails before extraction was one operation he was glad not to have to do.

Wedging the bulky nobs of the forceps under the shoe was another problem. Lewis needed something sharp to slide between the shoe and the hoof to help lift it. The most likely sharp object was nearby. Any one of the large daggers stuffed in the belts of either brother would do. Another test of Qamrani's persuasive talents. He did not even try. Instead, he ran to the kitchen and grabbed Faizah's favourite kitchen knife out of her hand and fled, drawing a burst of abuse and pipe smoke with him.

The knife worked, though Lewis was careful not to cut into anything. He now had enough space for the forceps to get a grip and prise the shoe off. He removes what remains of the outer sock, then the other used to pad the cavity. There had been some bleeding and peeling the sock away from the frog without wetting it would start the bleeding again. As the hoof needed washing before treatment, water was absolutely necessary.

A moist rag with only enough water to squeeze onto the sock is all Qamrani could offer. Proof to Lewis just how ridiculous this ban on water was. But he must make the most of what he has. After carefully peeling away the fabric from the frog, he inspects the damage. It was not good, but far better than if he had not put in the sock. Sand and grit that had passed through the material needs to be removed from the soft flesh. This becomes a flinching, slow process. When Lewis had finished, he looks around for Qamrani. He is nowhere to be seen, nor are the two older brothers. They most likely became bored, hot or hungry. If it were not for an open wounded hoof without a shoe, he could make his escape. But it would have to wait, and he begins preparing the nails for straightening.

A tap on his shoulder announces Qamrani's return carrying a small bowl.

"This for foot," he says continuing to knead the contents of the bowl.

"What is it?" asks Lewis, wary of putting anything onto the injury that is unfamiliar.

"Please, it will help," assures Qamrani handing the bowl to Lewis.

Lewis smells the dough-like contents and recognises the aroma of dates.

"Dates and what else?" he asks still concerned.

"Um, how you say, brrr…no boiled, boiled leaves of Eilejaan and softened Ghagha stems."

Lewis has a feel of the fibrous dough and another smell. "You sure?" he asks, looking into the young boy's eyes.

"It will make heal faster," he says with a nod.

Lewis has no choice but to trust the boy. He moulds the dough into a ball and presses it into the hoof cavity. Spade, who has been relatively calm and tolerant throughout the process, gives a snort and a nod. The sock used as a pad is unrolled and placed over the whole hoof to hold in the poultice and the shoe is nailed back on.

All that remains for Lewis to do is stay with Spade, keep him calm and massage his legs and back.

Qamrani watches on with his doleful eyes. All the time they have been together he has yearned to touch the animal. As Lewis runs his hands along Spade's back, Qamrani reaches out. Spade has become used to having the boy near, and unlike with his older brothers, has not shown any objection. Lewis watches as Qamrani's hand nears Spade's flesh then stops. Lewis gives him a nod to continue. Tentatively, his hand rests on the neck of Spade who turns his head towards the boy. A smile spreads across Qamrani's youthful face at being accepted. Lewis moves aside so Qamrani can take over stroking Spade's back. The nearby camels groan their protest.

"I hate camels," Qamrani mutters.

"Spade likes you. You want to ride him?" suggests Lewis.

Qamrani quickly removes his hand from Spade as if he'd got himself into something he should not have.

"This fella need to walk. He stand too long, and your medicine has made him more comfortable. "

Qamrani smiles that he has done something important.

"Ssp…Spade?" he questions.

"Yeah right. His name's Spade."

"Spade," repeats Qamrani. "As Salam alaykom, Spade." He adds with an introductory bow.

Lewis smiles back. "Come, you put a foot here," he says cupping his hands beside Spade.

Qamrani looks around to make sure no one is around to see. Only the camels have their eyes on him. He bends his leg and places a foot into Lewis' hands who then hoists him up and onto Spade's back. Spade gives a nod and a shuffle. Qamrani makes a move to get off thinking he is not welcome, but Lewis pats Spade's neck and pushes Qamrani into a better position.

Considering the horse's adverse reaction towards his brothers, acceptance fills Qamrani with joy. He bursts out into laughter.

Lewis unties the rope from the tent pole and steers Spade away from the camels. The movement under him makes Qamrani laugh more. He grabs onto Spade's mane as he's led in a wide circle. The laughter gets louder and more childlike. Enough to raise interest from inside the tent and Runmaiz and Jumaa come to see what the noise is all about.

Seeing the horse untied and walking away is enough for Runmaiz to raise his rifle and take aim. Jumaa quickly pushes the barrel of the gun down.

"You want to shoot your brother?' he warns.

Runmaiz is again dominated by his older brother. Unable to hold back his rage any longer he pulls the rifle away from Jumaa, raises it, and before Jumaa can do anything, fires a shot.

Qamrani's laughter is cut short. Lewis pulls on the rope to stop his horse and looks back. Runmaiz aimed high, missing all. But it was enough to send a ripple of fear through Qamrani. He jumps off the horse, grabs the rope out of Lewis' hand and obediently leads the horse and Lewis back to the tent. The sound of the rifle shot has brought Faizah, the Sheikh and A'isha out to see what was happening.

"Easy fellas," Lewis calls out with hands raised. "The

horse, he just needed to stretch his bloody legs, okay."

"Qamrani…go!" snaps Runmaiz and watches his young brother run to his mother. The Sheikh watches with interest to see what his older sons will do. A'isha is eyeing everyone to make sense of the scene. Her mind endlessly searches for any escape opportunity that may present itself.

Jumaa steps forward between his angry brother and Lewis. His hand is outstretched for the rope. Lewis gives it to him.

"The boy's not to blame, hey?" pleads Lewis. "All my fault."

But he's not understood, nor would they take any notice anyway.

Spade begins to get agitated again having the rope in the hands of Jumaa.

"Easy mate," whispers Lewis in an attempt at keeping his horse calm.

But Jumaa does not tie the rope to the tent post. He stands in front of Lewis and indicates he wants to get on Spade's back.

"You fix horse, now we can ride," Jumaa insists. Lewis looks to Qamrani for a translation.

Qamrani lowers his eyes. "He say, I ride so now can he…sorry, sir."

Lewis knows he has no choice and the two will ride sooner or later, so now will have to do. He goes to help Jumaa onto Spade when the Sheikh steps forward and orders a halt.

"Jumaa and Runmaiz, you will get your first ride tomorrow when you mount for the race." Without listening to any protests from his sons, he returns to the cool of the tent.

Jumaa calls Qamrani over and throws him the rope. "Make sure you tie the rope tight, Qamrani." He gives Lewis a fierce look before heading to the tent, grabbing Runmaiz's arm as he goes past for him to follow. Runmaiz has his rifle aimed at Lewis and pops his lips before he's dragged away.

It was a not-to-subtle hint that when the race is run, done and over, so could be Lewis' life.

*

Nighttime finally begins to suck the heat out of the air. Lewis is confident he's done all he can to give his horse every chance of surviving the race. But the refusal to allow Spade to drink continues to grate. The only food Spade's given is what the camels eat. The problem being, while it may be okay for the camels, the salty grass will only hasten dehydration and possibly bring on a bout of colic. Adding a further insult, the camels have been taken to a well at the base of the nearby hill to drink. The smell of water so close has Spade groaning and scratching the ground.

Lewis tries to comfort his horse as much as he can by stroking his neck, rubbing his nose and wiping tears from his eyes. But this act of reassurance is starting to wear thin. All Lewis can do is wish the following day will dawn as fast as possible. At least the race will be held early to escape the extreme heat of the day.

His pleading to sleep with Spade is ignored, and he's ordered back inside the tent. The moment his hands leave the twitching flesh of his horse is when Lewis cannot hold back. He quickly steps around the side of the tent to hide his tears.

Chapter 18
THE RACE

[Lewis]

Lewis is having a sleepless night as if the war still raged and it's the eve of another battle. On those occasions, sounds and images of home would invade his mind to help sweep away the fear of death. Then, as in so many other times of impending danger, Dreamtime spirits would visit. They would make him feel he was back in the land of his creation.

There were enough similarities to this foreign land to believe it. The arid landscape with its sparse vegetation, the intense heat of the sun, the extreme cold of the nights and some animals, insects and reptiles that were common to both lands…all comforting but for one serious omission…*his* songline! Chosen for him at the time of his creation, but distant from this foreign place. *Was it not meant to follow me?* He often thought. *Did my ancestral spirits refuse to cross the vast seas to this place of war? Have they deserted me? Have I deserted them?*

He opens his eyes and waits till they adjust to the darkness in the tent. The reality of his situation becomes unnervingly clear. The decision to desert the army to save Spade means he no longer has a home.

Morning breaks to another cloudless sky. Qamrani is up early to set the course for the race. He ties blue and red strips of fabric to three poles placed at equal distance from, and back to, the start/finish line. As the Bedouin have no unit of measurement, Qamrani rides a camel to decide the equal distances. Two hundred camel strides from the start to the first pole. A further two hundred strides between each and back to the start/finish. The total length of the square course is approximately one and a half imperial miles. The flat area chosen offers a clear view over the whole improvised circuit.

As this will be a race against time, the timer will be a tent post driven into the ground to act as a sundial and also the start/finish post. The distance the tip of its shadow moves for each ride will mark the time taken to complete the course. The shortest distance the shadow moves will determine the winner.

Due to the early start, the morning meal will be served beside the starting line. The Sheikh has settled down on scattered cushions to watch the proceedings. The carpets used to shade Spade now lay on the ground for the Sheikh's wife and the coffee she has delivered. A plate of dates, bread and yoghurt sits beside the steaming coffee pot. Accepting an invitation to watch the event, A'isha sits away from the start and beside the bemused camels.

The sight of a sweating, trembling and famished horse gives A'isha doubts he will last the day. If he dies, so does her chance of her freedom. She looks around for Lewis who is the only one not present. Unknown to her, he sits shackled and confined inside the tent for the duration of the race.

Sheikh Abdulla bin Rashidi announces that his middle son, Runmaiz, will ride first. Jumaa protests that he, being the oldest, deserves the first ride. The protest falls on deaf ears. Runmaiz, though, is happy to show his elation, for he, too, thought age would dictate in which order they rode. Now his expectation of winning has heightened.

Despite Runmaiz's eagerness to get on with the race, Spade continues to deter him from mounting. His father has strictly forbidden his desire to whip the horse into submission. Try as he may, Spade is the aggressor and Runmaiz cannot even get a hand on him. After some coaxing from Qamrani, the Sheikh relents and allows the release of Lewis to assist.

Already furious at the no water rule, then enraged further by being tied up and confined to the tent, gets a sharp refusal from Lewis. But the consequences of not helping play on his mind. Runmaiz would, sooner or later, use violence. It would take a long time to defeat Spade. He would become stressed, exhausted and further dehydrated. As the heat is already rising, Lewis concedes that the earlier they start the race, the better it will be for Spade. He yields to their request.

There's subdued emotion when Lewis and Spade come together again. The only cloud in the cloudless sky is the gloom hovering over both. Could this be the last day the pair will be together? Will Lewis never again sit on Spade's back? Or for Spade to feel his weight and the subtle instructions from his knees? Lewis thinks back to his last ride. It was days ago. Was that to be the last?

Lewis is checking Spade's foreleg and giving it a final massage before anyone mounts. Runmaiz, whose adrenalin has surged, prods Lewis with the stick he continues to carry. Spade spins his head around, forcing Runmaiz to retreat a pace.

"Okay, mate," Lewis whispers into Spade's ear. "You get this over pretty damn quick, hey? Then you drink, all right?"

Spade gives a snort, shakes his head and ends with a nod, not once but three times.

"Good boy, Spade. You can do this. I know you can. Think of Beersheba."

Lewis cannot delay the inevitable any longer. He stands and walks Spade in a half circle to face the start. The thought of jumping onto his back and riding off is tempting. But Jumaa is holding Runmaiz's carbine and has it aimed at them both. It's a chance not worth taking at this moment but one he will grab if the opportunity arises. He slides his hand up the rope to hold it firmly at the neck and steady Spade for the arrogant Bedouin to mount.

Mounting a horse with no saddle and who is standing rather than a camel that sits is unfamiliar to Runmaiz. With little to hold onto and a sweating, slippery horse, he misjudges the height and slides off, landing under the horse and on his backside. In a flurry of shuffling feet, he scrambles out from under Spade and away from the fidgeting hooves.

Qamrani laughs but is quickly silenced by his father. Jumaa is far too angry at not riding first to laugh, but cannot hide his delight at the spectacle.

Runmaiz takes his embarrassment out on Lewis with a swipe across the back with the stick. Spade reacts and is about to break from Lewis' grip on the rope in his defence, but Lewis manages to hold him steady.

Qamrani watches Lewis with his usual intensity, expecting a reaction. There is none. Lewis pushes against Spade's left side to straighten him up again. With one hand holding the rope, he cups the other as a stirrup. Runmaiz will need all the help on offer to throw a leg over the fifteen hand high Spade. He is confident that once on board, he can control the horse, but failing to mount a second time would shame him eternally. It takes all his willpower to accept the help of an infidel soldier.

Jumaa watches with keen interest. When it becomes his turn to mount, he cannot afford such dishonour.

A mix of awkwardness, loss of face and the hoisting hand of Lewis sees Runmaiz finally on top of Spade. He grabs a handful of Spade's mane to secure himself. When Lewis feels Runmaiz is well seated, he hands him the neck rope. Spade gives a half-hearted buck. Not enough to dislodge the unwanted intruder on his back, but to remind him it would not be difficult.

There's a need for Runmaiz to claim back some lost esteem. He takes control of the horse and steers Spade in several circles to get used to the feel of the horse beneath him. His experience riding camels shows as he gains more control over his mount. With legs wedged against

Spade's sides, he heads to the line drawn in the sand at the starting post.

The sun is still low, casting a long shadow from the sundial. All is quiet from the onlookers. Even the camels have stopped chewing. The Sheikh gets a nod from Runmaiz that he is as ready as he ever will be. Qamrani waits for his father's hand to drop. Runmaiz leans forward with his feet primed to kick Spade in the flanks. All eyes are on the Sheikh except for Lewis who is watching his horse with great concern. A'isha grasps her talisman, closes her eyes and whispers to herself a prayer for the horse. Finally, the Sheikh's hand drops. The spot at the tip of the shadow is marked and the race against time begins.

Despite only riding camels sidesaddle, Runmaiz shows a degree of skill. Spade picks up speed and accelerates from a canter to a gallop. The first leg is used to get used to the rhythm of the horse at a gallop. To Runmaiz's expectation, a camel's gate at full speed is the same as a horse at a gallop. By the time he reaches the first pole, his confidence is climbing. He swoops down without slowing and grabs the strip of red material. It will now be the colour he needs to pluck from the remaining posts. The blue ribbons must remain attached for his brother. A mistake in grabbing the wrong ribbon, or to have the correct one slip from your grip will be costly. The rider will need to stop, return to the pole, grab the right coloured material then build up speed again.

The race to the second pole is even faster. Runmaiz makes another clean grab of the red ribbon. But he can feel the horse under him beginning to tire and gives him a sharp kick.

At the starting line, all attention is on horse and rider as they turn toward the third pole. Jumaa glances down at the tip of the shadow projecting from the timing post. A frown creases his brow seeing the short distance it has progressed. Knowing he will be on a tiring horse, the chance of winning is becoming slight. He looks back up as his younger brother reaches the next pole and a smile eases Jumaa's worried expression. Runmaiz's overconfidence has resulted in a lapse in concentration and the third red ribbon slips out of his hand. He pulls back on the rope to bring Spade to a halt before turning him around for another try. He snatches at the red ribbon. It remains caught. In a fit of fury, he places a foot on the post and pulls harder. The force splits the wood leaving the blue ribbon dangling from its ragged edge.

Runmaiz is furious at himself and now needs to make up the time lost. After several solid kicks, Spade is struggling to get back to speed. Runmaiz looks to the finish line and those watching. Confident they cannot see, he removes the jagged stick he had shortened and hidden under his tunic. The sharp points where side shoots have broken off draws blood with each strike. But there is little acceleration. Runmaiz whips him harder. The cuts get deeper without any increase in speed. He throws the stick away before reaching the finish. Then makes a point of showing both hands on mane and rope to those watching.

Qamrani sticks a marker in the sand at the tip of the sundial shadow as Spade crosses the line. The bloodied side of the horse is now facing all those watching. Lewis' lingering anger now turns to utter rage at the sight of the flesh wounds. Adding further to Lewis' concerns, Runmaiz pulls Spade up far too quickly.

Lewis makes a move to run and grab Runmaiz with the intention of dragging him from his horse and giving him a beating. But Jumaa grabs him before he can manage two steps. Runmaiz rides back to the starting line. The bloody wounds are now on the far side and out of sight of those by the tent. Runmaiz flashes a brazen look at Lewis before swinging his leg over Spade's back and sliding to the ground. Lewis takes a step toward him with clenched fists, but a nudge from the barrel of a rifle stops him. Qamrani is quick to grab the neck rope and walks Spade off in a circle to bring him back to the start line. As he passes the hissing camels, A'isha notices the blood streaming down Spade's rump. She looks up, expecting an angry Lewis to remonstrate. But Lewis, having shrugged off Jumaa, stands slumped and forlorn. The heat is continuing to rise, and Lewis commits to getting this farcical race over as soon as possible.

Chapter 19

MAGIC CARPET RIDE

Jumaa Ayed studies the distance the shadow of the sundial has travelled. He expected it to be longer after his younger brother's problem at the third post. At least it has given him a slim chance. But when Qamrani delivers Spade to him, the possibility of beating his brother fades. The run has taken a lot out of the horse. Though there seems no discernible worsening of the damaged hoof, he's lathered up, breathing rapidly and dehydrated. But it's the lacerations to his rump that has Jumaa turn to his brother for an explanation.

"What have you done, brother? Did you beat this horse?" he asks suspiciously.

Runmaiz throws up his hands. "I know not of this," he says rather unconvincingly. Then points to Qamrani. "It was the last post that Qamrani put in the ground. It was broken making the ribbon hard to remove. The horse must have scraped it when I rode off."

"That is not true, Jumaa," pleads Qamrani.

Jumaa looks into his young brother's eyes and sees the pain of being unfairly blamed. Preferring to believe Qamrani over the questionable Runmaiz, he turns to his father to complain about the unfair tactics of his brother. Before he can say a word, the Sheikh raises a silencing hand and gives him a knowing nod. Nothing passes the keen eye of his father and Jumaa again feels there's more to this race than just winning a horse.

A'isha watches on with a sense of defeat. The horse she hopes to ride away on may not last another run. If that is to be, she tries to sort through the consequences. If he dies or is crippled, then there is no escape. There's a mutual hatred between her and camels so that option is out. She could be sold off to someone desperate enough to marry a mute. Or, as it now seems likely that Runmaiz will win the race, Jumaa is the least objectionable if she is to be his consolation prize.

But there is one thought that confuses her. *What will happen to the boy soldier? And why, with all problems I have, should I be worried about him?*

She looks up at hearing Lewis making a desperate plea to the Sheikh to end this madness. But all the gesturing, pointing and garbled words seem meaningless to the old man. Though, he does take a moment to look over the horse before instructing Jumaa to get ready for the next run without delay.

Qamrani looks to Lewis for some assurance that he believes he is not to blame for the cuts to his horse. But Lewis' only concern is for Spade and his pleading look goes unnoticed.

Jumaa has no doubt who inflicted the wounds. But there is doubt about the forlorn, dispirited and suffering horse waiting for him to mount. He considers relinquishing his ride and accepting defeat. But hanging over him is a lingering suspicion he sensed from his father. *This is not only a race for a horse, but a display of worthiness to be his rightful successor.* He feels all eyes on him. Wondering why he hesitates. *To not ride will show weakness. To ride may kill the horse.* He looks to Spade and feels his pain. Then to his brother with disgust. *I must not allow him to win so easily!*

Lewis can do nothing but accept that the race will continue despite his protests. The quicker it is over the better, so he holds the rope tight to steady Spade for Jumaa. Being taller than his younger brother, Jumaa mounts Spade on the first go. Runmaiz dismisses it as a stroke of luck and a tired horse. His arrogant confidence remains undiminished.

Lewis leans closer to his horse and whispers in his ear. "Follow your songline, Spade, them ancestral spirits of yours will look after you."

Qamrani marks the tip of the shadow and the run commences.

Like his brother, it takes time for Jumaa to get used to being on a running horse bareback. Even longer to get Spade up to a full gallop. Runmaiz looks down at the slow moving shadow and makes no attempt at hiding the smug smile on his face. Looking back up he sees Spade falter and appear disorientated rounding the first pole. His confidence at winning increases.

Lewis takes an anxious step forward but is nudged back by Runmaiz's carbine trained on him.

A'isha also shows concern and attempts to stand for a clearer view. A loud grunt and a fierce look from Faizah stops her. A nod to the earth emphasises her place is to sit and be quiet. A'isha is further resolved to get away from this woman with her pipe, constant murmurings and deadly stare. *If the horse is to die I will see it as punishment.*

Qamrani is not watching the horse. Whatever will happen he will see through Lewis' reactions. Already, he believes, by the intensity of Lewis' stare and his deep, barely audible murmuring, that he is communicating with his horse.

Lewis suddenly straightens up and raises a hand to shade his eyes. The change of expression on his face compels Qamrani to turn his attention to the race. To his amazement, the terrain has changed. He looks around at the others. Their lack of surprise is puzzling. They appear to be only interested in whether the horse will survive, not in the curving mound of rising sand that Spade is floating on.

Atop Spade, Jumaa is struggling to keep the horse in a straight line to the next pole, unaware of what is happening beneath them. In fact, in the unlikely event he ever did have control, it is now well and truly out of his hands. Also, seemingly, out of the control of Spade. The bounce of the faltering gallop has smoothed. The sound of hooves beating divots in the sand fades as a gossamer-like mist enshrouds them, sending Jumaa into a trance. His last recollection is the sensation of floating on a magic carpet.

Apart from Lewis, the others are blind to what is happening. All they see is a faltering horse about to lose a race. Even Qamrani is lulled into a dream-like state. Lewis closes his eyes to the real world and wills the spirits that have followed him from his ancestral beginnings to show themselves.

Spade carries his rider into a diverging universe. Jumaa and those watching, apart from Lewis, see only flat sand and a race continuing. Blue ribbons continue to be plucked from each post and a tiring horse is struggling to finish.

But Spade is not tiring. Instead, he floats on the mist of Dreamtime images that follow his newly discovered songline. Lewis continues his undertone singing. His head lowers, and a smile dissolves the worry from his face.

Then, as if time itself had lapsed, Spade, with Jumaa on his back, crosses the finish line. Qamrani, alert and oblivious to the spiritual happenings, pokes a stick in the ground at the point of the shadow. No one questions how the horse ran, stayed on course or even survived. It was now all a matter of fact. The horse ran, all blue ribbons were gathered, it finished and whatever happened in between is somehow lost in time.

Lewis opens his eyes and moves to greet his horse, ignoring Runmaiz who is staring at the markers in the sand that will determine who was fastest.

"Water! He's done what you ask. Now he needs water," Lewis calls in desperation.

Qamrani looks to his father for permission. Instead, the old man whispers into his ear. Qamrani straightens up with a confused look but bows his obedience. He first approaches his mother with instructions to take the girl back into the tent. Then, catching up with Lewis, he attempts to steer him also into the tent.

Lewis snatches his arm away and points to Spade. "He needs water! Don't you understand?"

"It will be done," replies Qamrani taking hold of Lewis' arm once again. "I assure you as Allah is my witness, I will have your horse watered, but you must stay in the tent for now."

Dumbfounded, Lewis looks back to Spade then to the Sheikh with pleading eyes. But the steely expression on the face of the old man dismisses any argument. Lewis looks back at Qamrani. He has trusted this boy and studies him for a sign he will not go against his word.

"Please," urges Qamrani. "You must go into the tent now."

Accepting that any resistance will only prolong his horse's agony, he joins A'isha as they both enter the tent. There is no exchange between them. Each is caught up in their own distraction.

Meanwhile, Jumaa has tied Spade to the tent pole and is walking back to his father shaking the remnants of haze from his mind. He joins Runmaiz studying the start and finish marks in the sand. The distance the shadow travelled for each ride appears very similar. But Runmaiz only sees what he wants to see.

"I have won, big brother," he boasts.

"How can you say that, Runmaiz?" questions Jumaa pointing to the ground. "Only a measurement will determine who wins."

Sheikh Abdulla bin Rashidi looks at his two oldest sons with a questioning intensity. He looks back to make sure the two newcomers under his care are out of sight then calls Jumaa and Runmaiz to his side.

"Runmaiz, you state, with utmost certainty, that you have won without a measure taken," their father says rising to his feet. "And Jumaa, you show uncertainty by asking for measures to be taken."

The Sheikh steps up to the first mark made in the sand. His eyes follow the route the shadow had taken to the last mark in the sand.

Without raising his eyes, he says, "Runmaiz, your confidence, though touched with youthful arrogance, is worthy of a future leader."

Runmaiz slaps his chest with one hand and raises the other to give thanks to Allah for the win.

"But Jumaa," he continues. "Your request that a measure to be taken is a sign of consideration and fairness."

Runmaiz's presumptuous smile fades and his raised hand slowly lowers. Jumaa remains motionless.

Without hesitation and with one swipe of his sandalled foot, the Sheikh wipes out the marks in the sand.

Both sons look stunned at their father's action. Their mouths slump open. The only sound is a slight gurgle from Runmaiz throat.

"I have one more test for you," adds the Sheikh sitting back down on his cushions. He beckons the two young men to come closer.

"You have now both been on the back of the horse. You have both ridden the horse. You have both left a mark in the subconscious mind of the horse. That horse is of pure Arabian blood. An animal of high intelligence and one that cannot be easily fooled. He will decide who will be his owner."

Both boys start stuttering to get words of protest out but are stopped by their father's raised hand.

"The horse is desperate for water. It will be provided. But at a distance. The smell of water will draw the horse to it, and nothing will stop it." He pauses. "Except for loyalty."

The brothers look at each other confused.

"You will both call the horse. If it returns to one of you without quenching its thirst, you will then become the horse's new master and next in line to be Sheikh of this clan."

He leans back to relish the bewildered silence of his older sons.

Finally, Jumaa finds the words to speak. "Father? What if the horse does not come back to either of us?"

The old man weighs up his response. "That is of no concern to me…only to you."

Chapter 20
THE LOYALTY TEST

[A'isha]

Faizah fills and lights her pipe and orders A'isha to go back to her chores. Before long the kitchen area hums with the old woman's constant mutterings. It's hard to tell if she's angry or not, for it seems a permanent affliction. But wasting a morning watching men and their inane goings-on has soured her expression even more.

A'isha is more dispirited than enraged and takes out her frustration by crushing a bowl of cardamom seeds used to soften the bitter taste of coffee. She could use a seed or two to quell the bitterness she carries. The horse has not died, but unaware of the Sheikh's latest decree, she believes the race has decided the horse's new owner. It will most likely be sold or gifted to win the hand of a wife. She turns her head to where the camels sit outside the tent. As well a mutual hatred, she finds them slow, smelly and hard to ride. But with all other option gone, they may now be the only way out of her predicament.

[Lewis]

Lewis continues to protest as Qamrani leads him to the men's sleeping quarters.

"At least let me see that he gets water," he pleads.

Qamrani ignores him and proceeds to rummage

through Runmaiz clothes. The one's he thinks would fit the best he hands to Lewis and motions for him to change into them.

"What the bloody…what's this about?" asks a baffled Lewis giving the clothes a curious look. "My horse needs water, and all you can do is give me your bloody brother's clobber!"

"The horse will get water without delay, I assure you," replies Qamrani feeling the strange tingle every time he looks into the eyes of the soldiers. "But first you must prove your loyalty of your horse."

"Loyalty? My loyalty is to see my horse gets water now!"

Qamrani thrusts the clothes at Lewis again. "Come! Do not waste time. Your horse is suffering. You must put on!"

Lewis shakes his head in disbelief. "Is this a bloody joke? You want me to dress up just so my horse can get water?"

"It is my father's order that you wear these. Your horse does not get water until."

Lewis looks over his shoulder and thinks of Spade… exhausted, thirsty and suffering. If wearing the clothes is the only way Spade can get some water, he'll do it.

"How do I put them on?" he asks Qamrani.

"You must first take off all your clothes," Qamrani says showing some urgency by starting to help unbutton his shirt.

"I can bloody well do it," snaps Lewis, but fumbles with the buttons in his haste.

Lewis' uniform lies in a pile on the floor. He stands

looking down at his new attire. Camel hide sandals cover his feet. His body is draped in a loose-fitting full-length slightly soiled and frayed thobe. A button is missing at the neck. A white scarf is loosely wrapped around his head and tied at the back. To finish the outfit off, Qamrani takes off his own belt and ties it around Lewis' waist.

Qamrani takes one more look before making a few adjustments. Satisfied, he ushers Lewis out of the tent and to where Spade is languishing.

As soon as Runmaiz and Jumaa see Lewis in Bedouin clothes they're confused and mystified.

"What is this, Qamrani?" Runmaiz snaps, still angered by his father's strange instructions. Then, recognising his adversary is wearing his own clothes, his anger turns to confounded rage.

"It is our father's wish," replies Qamrani taking Lewis to the Sheikh's side. "You stay. I get water now."

Finally, this is what Lewis has been waiting to hear. But when Qamrani heads off into the desert with two water-filled goat skins, he's left totally mystified.

"Where you bloody going?" calls out Lewis. "My horse is here, not over there!"

The Sheikh beckons Lewis to calm down with a look that calls for patience.

But nothing will calm Lewis. He sees Spade agitated by the smell of water and Jumaa is struggling to hold him back from chasing after it.

Qamrani reaches the first post of the race, places the two skins of water down on the sand and waves back to the tent.

Jumaa gets a nod from his father and releases his

hold on the rope. Spade immediately starts galloping toward the sweet smell of water. Lewis is still confused but delighted that his horse will soon drink.

When Spade is a third of the way to the quenching water, the Sheikh gives his sons approval to begin.

Runmaiz is first to call out. The word in Arabic is strange and drowned out by Jumaa's command. A battle of who is the loudest begins with the words that will turn the horse around. Neither of then, of course, has ever known the horse's name, nor any words in English that the horse may understand. The scene is becoming comical…but not to Lewis.

"What dem fellas doing?' he asks, looking back at the Sheikh. "They're bloody trying to stop my horse from drinking!"

With no response from the old man, Lewis starts calling out himself. "Go, Spade," he yells. "You no listen to dem fellas. You go drink that water."

The sound of Lewis' voice, above the confused foreign babble of the brothers, reaches Spade's ears and he stops. So does the yelling and calling out from the tent. Runmaiz breaks into a smile of conquest. Jumaa is nodding and beckoning the horse to come to him.

Lewis stands dumbfounded. "No!" he calls out. "No Spade…go to the water."

But the more Lewis calls out; the more Spade turns his back on the desperately needed fluid. The years of trust and companionship, the calling and obeying of orders and the respect they have for each other is overwhelming. Spade turns and takes his first stride in the direction of his friend's voice.

Both brothers believe the horse is returning to them. With more frantic waving of arms, they step away from each other so there will be no confusion about whom the horse goes to.

Lewis calls out one last time to try and change his horse's mind and for it to go back to the water.

"No Spade! Go back! Go back!"

The charge to Beersheba clouds Spade's mind. Lewis' call to 'go back, go back' sounds like the screaming throng of charging Light Horsemen calling out 'attack, attack'. Spade accepts the challenge and kicks into a charging gallop.

The speed with which he arrives at the tent sends the two brothers, their father and the camels scattering to avoid a collision with a horse in full flight.

But Lewis stands firm and watches Spade skid to a halt at his feet.

Qamrani was not far behind with both water bags slopping as he runs. As soon as he had seen the horse stop and turn back from the water, it was as he prophesied— the voice of the soldier would prevail over thirst. Delight shows on his face that neither of his brothers triumphed.

Lewis grabs one of the water bags while Spade sniffs at the strange clothes his master is wearing. If they were meant to fool him, it failed. Lewis grabs his horse's head and places the open water bag under his nose. With a snort and permission to drink, Spade tastes his first water in days. The second water-filled goat skin is held back to allow Spade to digested the first load. He now needs a short walk to calm down so the second drink will be less rushed. Lewis starts to lead Spade away from the tent, but the cocking of a carbine brings him to a halt.

Lewis hands the neck rope to Qamrani rather than agitate Runmaiz any more than he is. Qamrani understands what's required and leads Spade off for a slow walk around the camp.

[A'isha]

A'isha looks up from her bowl of cardamom as Qamrani leads a more relaxed-looking Spade into view. Water dripping from his wet nose is a relief to see. Her mind starts to race. She looks at the murmuring old woman showing no interested in anything but her bread making. A'isha looks back, expecting others to follow. They don't. It takes only an instant to see this as her last chance to grab the horse and ride as fast and as far as she can. The camels sit tethered and without their saddles. She could be some distance away before they can organise themselves to chase after her.

The bowl on her lap is flung aside scattering seeds and crushed herb over Faizah. She looks up startled, spilling her bread mixture and letting the pipe fall from her mouth. A'isha is on her feet and dashing towards the horse. The freshly brewing coffee pot is sent flying, spilling its contents onto the fire. Faizah is more concerned about spilt coffee, wasted cardamom and bread mix than chasing after the fleeing A'isha.

Qamrani's frailty makes it easy for A'isha to push him aside. He stumbles and falls to the ground. She grabs the rope as it slips from his hand. Then, lifts up her tunic, flings her leg over Spade's back, and with a kick in his ribs, rides off into the desert.

Chapter 21
ENTER THE RENEGADES

Qamrani struggles to his feet in a panic. Losing the horse under his control grips at his heart and stifles his voice from calling for help. His pulse is racing. All he has left is to give chase. He'll run for as long as he can. If he fails to catch up with the girl and the horse, he would rather die in the desert than face humiliation from his family. An even greater fear is the curse that the soldier will assuredly cast upon him.

Faizah is the one to raise the alarm. Her concern is not for the horse or the girl, but for her youngest son thrown to the ground.

Lewis had already started to react to the sound of the coffee pot and other objects crashing to the ground. A quick glance around the cooking quarters proves his worse fear. The girl is gone! Images of her riding off with his horse from the Light Horse camp flash in his mind. He's first to reach the front of the tent followed by Runmaiz and Jumaa. Qamrani, Spade and the girl are nowhere in sight. Faizah is screaming for her son and pointing to her right. Lewis runs back to the rear of the tent in the hope of seeing his horse from there. All he sees is the Sheikh standing in wonderment at what is going on. He rushes to the far end of the tent, upsetting the camels. The thought of jumping on one is tempting, but the time needed to untie it and get it on its feet is time wasted. He studies the ground for tracks left by Spade. They are easy to spot, as are the running steps of the boy following. Lifting his eyes, he spots Qamrani before he disappears behind the distant hill. He hitches up the unfamiliar thobe to free his legs and runs in a loping stride to catch up with him.

Faizah is pointing to her right and screaming out instructions to her older sons. Confused, Runmaiz is waving his rifle around and aiming at anything. Jumaa rushes to mount one of the camels. As he's untying it, he looks towards the hill and sees the distant figure of Lewis in his flowing white thobe.

"Runmaiz!" he calls out. "Come quick and follow me on a camel."

Lewis is in full stride as he approaches the hill. Qamrani and Spade are still out of sight. He blindly rounds a sharp crevice at the edge of the hill. The speed he's worked up makes it impossible to avoid colliding into the stationary Qamrani. The boy has the wind knocked out of him and is sent crashing to the ground, followed by Lewis tripping over him. Lewis jumps to his feet and turns to release a violent outburst on the stunned Qamrani.

Qamrani struggles to regain his breath as he points into the desert. Lewis looks to where he's pointing. It takes a moment to adjust his eyes to the glare and haze. A blurred, shimmering shape is all he can make out. As he's about to continue the chase, Qamrani calls out.

"They…come…back."

Lewis looks to the boy then back to the shape. The single shimmering image is now separating. He strains his eyes to focus as Qamrani struggles to his feet. Through younger eyes, he has a clearer picture of the approaching images. He starts backing up and calls for Lewis to follow. Lewis looks at him and sees fear in the boy's eyes. On looking back, the distant images have defined into five shapes.

Qamrani continues to step back and just avoids another collision as Jumaa rounds the corner on his camel. Runmaiz is not far behind and also has to pull hard on the reins to stop. Lewis looks back at the brothers on their saddle-less camels. They too are now looking to where Qamrani is pointing and the approaching figures. All that Jumaa, Runmaiz, Qamrani and Lewis can do now, is wait for their arrival.

Five figures on horseback take shape. A relieved Lewis sees, among them, Spade with the girl on his back. But his relief is short-lived. The other four are in uniform.

Even though one wears a slouch hat, they are not of the Australian Light Horse. Despite the undisciplined mix in their appearance, Lewis recognises them as mounted Yeomanry. He's come across then a few times as they form part of the British mounted forces. For some reason, he recalls, they always showed a bit of antagonism towards the Light Horse. But something's not right with this bunch. They're not regular Yeomanry. They're renegades. When it became clear the war was about to end, some broke away from their regiments to form small packs. They roamed the desert looting and creating havoc among the Bedouin. They concentrated on small, displaced camps, such as the one on the other side of the hill.

To Lewis, they are no more than crooks. Out to profit from the spoils of war. And profit they will by turning him in as a deserter.

A'isha is continuing to kick and lash out at her captors in her furious best. If she had a voice, it would surely be heard all over the desert.

As soon as the group reach those waiting, A'isha is unceremoniously pushed off Spade and sent to the ground. Qamrani goes to help her up, but her kicking feet fend him off. Her raging disappointment of another failed escape attempt could not be clearer. She gets to her feet, gives a fierce glare back at her interceptors before dusting herself off.

The one exhibiting an air of being the leader kicks his horse a step closer to the small group. His men cover him with rifles raised. Jumaa suggests Runmaiz lower his.

"Shall we all return to your camp?" the leader says in a rather pompous English accent. "I assume it is nearby as two of you are on foot." There is no disguising a hint of a threat to anyone who may challenge him.

The slow walk back to the camp is in silence. Jumaa and Runmaiz lead the way on their camels followed by Qamrani. A'isha hangs back to keep some distance between her and the camels. Lewis keeps nudging her forward to show his anger towards her. Lewis then finds himself nudged forward by one of the horsemen.

Lewis is unsure what he can do with this new and

unwanted situation. Though, for the moment, he's thankful Spade is back with him.

The Sheikh and his wife are waiting at their tent as the group approach. Qamrani runs to his mother, who is pleased to see her young son returned unharmed, though slightly soiled. But she is still angry and not in the least interested in more unwanted visitors. She begins to dust sand off her son, but he steps back from her. Taking advantage of the fact that the horsemen are showing little interest in him for the moment, he sidles off into the tent.

The Sheikh welcomes the visitors with a bow and a touch to his forehead.

"Ahlan wa Sahlan," he offers. Then adds, "Assalamu Alaikum." Suggesting peace be with you in an attempt at easing the threat from raised rifles.

The leader dismisses the Sheikh's welcome with a disrespectful wave of the hand, appearing more interested in checking out his new surroundings. One of his men dismounts and proceeds to search for anyone else who may be around. He starts behind the tent to stop anyone who may be hiding inside from escaping. Finding only the remaining tethered camels, he enters the tent. A moment later the sound of a scuffle comes from within. The leader places his hand on his revolver while another aims his rifle at the tent flap. Steered out by his ear is Qamrani and thrust towards his mother. The leader gives the boy a questioning look. When told there are no others inside, he orders all weapons collected. Runmaiz shows some resistance to handing over his rifle. His father suggests with a nod that he obey. He and Jumaa are told to dismount and checked for hidden weapons. The older boys had removed their belts for the race and carry no daggers or pistols. Neither does the Sheikh or his wife. Lewis raises his arms to show he also carries no weapons.

The horses are becoming fidgety and nervous with the camels so close—a reason why some forces chose camels over horses in battle. They're led behind the tent to join the others.

The family group, including A'isha and Lewis, are now grouped together. The leader takes his time studying each in turn. Lewis has managed to edge himself back behind the taller Jumaa. The Arab clothes he now wears could be his salvation. He has dark skin like a Bedouin, a stubble of a beard, the look of a desert dweller and his sandalled feet show a roughness that a white man would rarely have.

Tempting fate, Lewis edges out from behind Jumaa for a clearer view of those still on horseback. An uncomfortable feeling comes over him. It's not so much the threat these men pose to him or the family; it's a searching pressure that has entered his mind and body. A feeling felt only once before…at the waterhole. His head begins to spin as he senses an intensive examination of him. He looks through clouded eyes to the fourth member of the group resting on his horse a little back from the others. His cold, dark stare feels as though he has seen through Lewis' disguise and is probing him from the inside.

This invasive connection breaks when the leader dismounts. The Sheikh again bows. "I am Sheikh

Abdullah bin Rashidi el Umbarak, and this is my family." As his dizziness and the external pressure subsides, Lewis becomes aware, much to his surprise, that the Sheikh spoke English all the time.

The leader replies with an impolite smirk. "Yes… well…Sheikh Abdullah, where is your offering of hospitality? Do you not greet desert travellers with nourishment and refreshment?"

The Sheikh immediately bows his apology and turns to his wife to prepare food and drink. She is in much need of tempering her anger, made worse when prompted to have A'isha assist. She looks to her husband who gives her a 'do-as-they-say' look. One of the men escorts them to the kitchen. Another proceeds to collects all the reins to take the horses to water. He waits for the fourth member to dismount. He continues to show interest in Lewis. Then, with an unnerving grin of discovery, he spits out whatever he chewed, slides off his horse and hands over the reins.

Spade is about to join the other horses as they're led to the water hole at the base of the hill. But, as he passes, the leader grabs the neck rope and stops him. A thoroughbred Arab horse would make a suitable replacement for his current worn-out steed. He reaches out to stroke Spade's nose. Spade snatches his head back. The leader persists. With a tight hold on the neck rope, he slides his hand down Spade's nose again. The white marking between Spade's eyes was always covered with boot polish so as not to be a target for the enemy to aim at. Now, after days of sweating, the boot polish is wearing off. The leader rubs his fingers together and smells them.

He gives a suspicious glance back at the gathered family before further examination. He recognises the neck rope as army issue. The army issue sock over the front right hoof brings on a bewildered smile. After a pause, he slides his hand along the tense, lean body of Spade and over his bloodied rump. The leader frowns as the wounds are fresh and the blood is yet to congeal. He walks around to the other side of Spade. His frown turns to a smile of confirmation as he slaps the arrow branding on his rump. He nods for Spade to join the others at the waterhole, satisfied he has seen all that's needed.

Lewis fears what this means. The inverted arrow that brands all horses of the Light Horse is proof of British Forces ownership.

This man be bloody suspicious now, I bet. Even if he accepts these Bedouin came across Spade and took ownership, I'm bloody sure he'll claim him. He'll say he's returning him to the army. But my bet is he'll become the new mount under this fella.

The leader takes another questioning look at those gathering before him. Knowing Spade is an army horse is one thing, seeing the army sock over his hoof is something else. It's a link to the owner. And by all signs, a very recent link.

Deciding, for the moment, not to pursue this further, the leader accepts the invitation to enter the tent for refreshments.

Chapter 22
TROUBLE BREWS

[Lewis]

Lewis, the Sheikh and his three sons are corralled under guard into the main section of the tent. A cold chill ripples down Lewis' spine. There is no way they will not see his discarded uniform lying on the floor of the male sleeping quarters. A quick glance, so as not to draw attention to where he's looking, leaves Lewis puzzled. His uniform is gone. Instead, standing and looking as innocent as a kitten is Qamrani.

That boy is a strange one for sure. He risk a lot to hide my uniform.

The Leader of the group takes it upon himself to recline on the plumpest cushions reserved for the Sheikh. The one who had taken the horses to water returns and flops down beside him. The third member of the group stands guard at the tent entrance. His cheeks bulge with a fresh mouthful of khat leaves. His eyes remain fixed on Lewis. The fourth remains in the kitchen watching over Faizah and A'isha.

The Sheikh offers to share the shisha pipe but it's refused. A rejection that is ungrateful and adds to the Sheikh's concern.

The leader introduces himself in a rather imperious manner. "I am captain Wiltshire-Smythe of the fourth

Yeomanry unit of the British Cavalry. This is Corporal Ramasamy Singh," he indicates with a nod to the khat-chewing guard. "Formerly of the Indian Imperial Forces, and a man of many intriguing skills." With a dismissive nod to his left, he adds. "…and private Gilbert Mashinter."

He takes a white silk kerchief from his sleeve and dabs at the sweat from his jowls. "And Sheikh?" he asks, showing more interested in his kerchief, "…is your English good enough to converse as my Arabic is not."

"A little," utters the Sheikh in a hushed tone.

"And your sons? They too speak English?"

"Only youngest," he says indicating with a nod in Qamrani's direction.

Lewis looks on faking ignorance of the English language.

The captain takes a moment to glance around the tent to further weigh up the situation.

"That is a rather handsome horse your daughter was riding. Do you have more like that?"

Private Mashinter, who led the horses to the rear of the tent, leans over to his captain and whispers in his ear. "I see, only camels and the one horse."

The Captain gives a hint of a nod and presses his kerchief to his top lip as Faizah and A'isha enter the tent.

"Oh, and this is sergeant, H. J. Claverdon," informs the captain, throwing a glance at the man following.

Faizah places a pot of sweet-smelling tea in the middle of the circle of men. A survivor of A'isha's destructive escape. Beside it, A'isha places a plate of cold flatbread and dates. Immediately the private grabs a handful of dates and bread. His captain ignores the display of disrespect, choosing to scan each of the Bedouin as they watch in horror the private's guzzling antics.

Lewis has been studying each of the intruders while maintaining a sheepish expression.

He sees the Captain as a bloated Englishman who refuses to acknowledge the heat of the desert. His uniform, most likely stolen, is a size too small for him. Buttons are stretching the thread they are sewn on with. His ruddy cheeks are bulging and his eyes water from a buttoned up collar that's causing his neck flesh to overflow. Under his sunburnt bulbous nose is a full moustache with a waxed twirl at each end. His slouch hat that differs from those worn by the Light Horse sits on the ground beside him. Unashamedly, his ill-fitting costume is an assemblage of various parts of uniforms either stolen or removed from the dead. All with the intention of promoting himself as someone of a rank higher than he could ever hope to equal.

Lewis judged the private as a nasty piece of work. Of similar age, scrawny with long, matted unwashed hair that is likely to harvest enough nutrition to feed a family of monkeys. He has a sour expression that not even the tea would sweeten. He has crust on his sleeve from the occasional wipe of his oozing nose. His shoulders slump, dragging his head down with them. His eyes flit from one object to another as if taking in an inventory of what to steal. A smile at anything of value shows teeth, or those still managing to secure a footing in diseased gums, are as grimy as his finger nails. In Lewis' opinion he would be a loose cannon in any unit and most likely the reason for his discharge.

The sergeant, Lewis feels, is a lesser problem for him that he could be for A'isha. He has not left her side, nor has his greedy gaze stopped feeding on her looks. If he weren't English, he'd pass as a beer-swilling German wrestler with more brawn than brains. His face has seen many a fight and his nose many a location. He has a scar running the length of his left cheek, that was, if at all, crudely stitched. The eye at the top of the scar most likely saw the injury coming and was the last sight it had. It's now half closed in a wicked twitching wink due to nerve spasms. His uniform is half British, half Ottoman and topped by a grey covered Bashlik helmet. The jacket still has epaulettes marking the rank of, not a sergeant, but a Mülâzim-i evvel, or first lieutenant. The previous dead owner had achieved far higher rank than a sergeant.

The corporal standing guard is the one Lewis finds most curious and worrying. Beside the unexplained and unnerving experience he got from him earlier, he's the only one in the correct uniform of the Indian Imperial Forces. The large, loose turban exaggerates his rather small head sitting atop a long thin neck. His body also seems lost in the folds of the loose jacket and the weighty bandolier across his chest. His khat-filled cheeks bulge and escaping juices dribble from his thin-lipped mouth. Flickering eyelids and twitching fingers are the minor symptoms of the drug known as Arabian tea. Something Lewis and his regiment were warned against in their health lectures. But most curious—and definitely not standard Indian Imperial Forces uniform—is the iron horseshoe hanging from his neck and horseshoe nails bent as rings on each finger of both hands. The drawing power the horseshoe has on Lewis again has him feeling light-headed. Could it be, that the strange projection emanating from Spade's lost shoe in the desert, was a warning of things to come?

This rapid appraisal is enough for Lewis to come to the blunt conclusion…*them fellas are bloody bad!*

The captain's slap to the private's head halts his gorging and allows the disgusted and bewildered Sheikh to instruct A'isha to pour the tea.

"Your daughter is pleasing to the eye, Sheikh. What is her name?"

Lewis raises his eyes wondering what his response will be as no one knows her name.

"She takes her mother's name, Faizah," answers the Sheikh without hesitation.

Clever, thinks a relieved Lewis.

"And where, Faizah, where were you riding to in such a hurry on a horse with no saddle and bleeding?"

"She has no voice," says the Sheikh with a shrug of his shoulders and waving a hand in front of his mouth. He pushes her headscarf up to show the tattoo on A'isha's brow.

"Ahhh, what a pity for someone so…" His voice trails off as he's handed a glass of tea.

The tea is excessively sweet. So much so the captain grimaces as the sweetness makes it hard to swallow, leaving the hot liquid to blister the roof of his mouth.

A'isha hides her delight. But her action of sabotaging the tea lights a fuse in the captain. His pompous aplomb crumbles. He places the glass of tea down then stiffens up with a serious expression. He cannot continue his charade of petty civility any longer.

"That horse belongs to British forces." He pauses to make sure his statement is clearly understood. "I'm curious. How did you come by it and do you know the whereabouts of its rider?"

While the Sheikh considers a response, Runmaiz reacts with a flick of his eyes towards Lewis. It does not go unnoticed.

The captain decides not to wait for whatever answer the Sheikh comes up with. His suspicion of a cover-up is confirmed. A look at the faces looking back at him brings on a smile. As far as he's concerned, there's no point in rushing to his intentions so soon. There will be plenty of time for that and food and shelter from the hot sun is not to be wasted. He returns to his civil persona, picks up the now tempered glass of tea, blows across its surface to cool it further, and raises it in a toast.

"Sheikh, to your kind hospitality." He takes a sip and places the glass back on the ground. "Now, we have travelled far and are in need of shade and rest. If you could be so kind and extend your hospitality, my men and I will remain here until nightfall. We will then be on our way."

The Sheikh spreads his hands wide. "As you wish. Rest, and I'll arrange food and water for your journey."

Lewis understands the Sheikh does not want trouble, but allowing them to stay is, without doubt, what he'll get.

Chapter 23
IRON VERUS DJINN

The captain demonstrates his superiority over his men by issuing them orders while he reclines on cushions and picks at the remnants of bread and dates on the platter before him.

The private has the job of watching over Spade and the other horses behind the tent. He sits with a dismal expression in the lengthening shade picking date skins from his rotten teeth and flicking them at the camels.

The sergeant is in the kitchen, having taken it upon himself to continue watching over A'isha and Faizah. To keep the old woman busy he orders her to make more bread for himself and their onward journey. A'isha does not wait for Faizah to ask for help. She'll do anything to occupy her mind so she can ignore the endless ogling of the sergeant. It's not only his salacious leer but the eerie feeling she has that there's something familiar about him.

The Indian corporal continues his watch over the males of the family that have been grouped together in the men's quarters. The corporal's dark, cold, steely eyes have a peacefulness about them. But no one under his gaze has any doubts that behind this pacifying veneer is a brutal desperado. A ruthless man who would not think twice about slitting any one of their throats.

Lewis has taken on a submissive, wide-eyed look of fear. But behind this veneer is a military mind trying to figure how to get out of this situation. As he, Aisha and the clan are now under armed guard there is no doubt of the renegades' intentions. They intend to ransack the camp, steal everything of value including Spade. And they would not hesitate to kill anyone who tries to stop them…if not all.

Lewis sits with his head bowed feeling the Indian corporal's eyes on him. Once or twice he had fought beside the Indian forces when they were on the same side. But this is not one of those occasions. This man and his gang are the enemy. In Lewis' mind, the war is not over. He must revert to being a cunning, well trained and experienced soldier.

His initial thought is to use the two brothers as a shield to get to the corporal and overpower him. But with the other three armed and out of sight, it could be risky. While he had no love for the older sons, he wished them no harm. Though, come sunset when the father's protection ends, Lewis is sure that at least one of the sons would not hesitate in revealing his identity.

[A'isha]

I try to get Faizah to look at me, but she continues to avoid eye contact. We need to work together to protect ourselves, but she is less friendly now than before. Does she blame me for bringing these men here?

This man who looks at me makes my skin crawl. He has removed his helmet, and his hairless head oozes sweat. He honks like a pig through his misshaped nose and twitches like a camel with a hundred fleas in its ear. His sweat-stained uniform reeks of himself, and his fat, blotched, unhealthy face is a clue to the rest of him. Someone so offensive to the eye should indeed stay in one's memory, but not mine. Yet there is something about him that, I fear, binds us.

A'isha's attempt to remember what, if any, connection there is to this man is suddenly interrupted. In a flurry of lost patience, the private bursts into the kitchen space and takes a kick at a basket of dates.

"Why do I always get the bloody boring jobs?" he bemoans to his sergeant in a broad cockney accent. "I hate bloody camels. All they do is splutter, chew and spit. If it be up to me I say shoot 'em all now, not later."

Sergeant Claverdon gives him scant attention, having learnt long ago to ignore the incessant complaining of the private.

"And I'm still bloody hungry!"

Faizah is sitting with legs crossed and her back to him. He slaps her on the shoulder. "Hey, you!" he calls to her. "You lot got anything other than dates to eat? I hate bloody dates. Ever since I've been in this bloody country, all I see are bloody dates."

Faizah continues to ignore him.

"Hey! I'm talking to ya!" he calls out with a heavier slap to the back of her head. It dislodges her scarf. She ignores him and calmly corrects it.

In an attempt to stop further torment of the old woman, A'isha tears off a piece of flat bread and offers it to the private.

"Well, well," he says with eyes lit up. "And what else can this little beauty offer?"

Without hesitation, private Mashinter grabs her hand and pulls her to him.

A'isha snatches her hand back, throws the bread into his face then follows up with a mouthful of spit.

This unleashes his uncontrollable anger. He turns on A'isha with a slap across the face and another attempt at pulling her to him. Her struggle proves she is stronger than he expected and he wraps his arms around her in a bear hug. The feel of her body struggling against him entices him to try for a kiss. He pulls her scarf aside to bare her neck. Before his lips have a chance to meet her flustered flesh, he's wrenched aside by the sergeant.

"She's mine first," he bellows.

With a heavy shove he sends the private stumbling over the tea and coffee pots. Failing to keep his balance, he falls into the fire and onto the hot metal plate the bread is baking on.

The resulting crashing, banging and screaming of the private, alerts everyone inside the tent.

First to hear is Corporal Ramasamy Singh. He stops chewing and turns his head toward the confused sounds. Lewis also heard the commotion and got the reaction from the Indian he was expecting. In a split second he pushes aside Jumaa and Runmaiz and dives at the corporal as if grounding a runaway steer. The two crash to the ground in a frantic struggle, sending the older brothers out of the way of flying fists and feet. The Indian manages to grab Lewis' head in his iron-encrusted hands and turns it so their eyes meet. Lewis immediately feels his head drain of understanding as he locks onto the flame-red eyes of the corporal. He begins to lose energy as if all his goodness and ancestral spirits are being sucked from his mind and body. The corporal gains control of his carbine and raises it to smash the stock into Lewis' head. He's stopped by the young Qamrani jumping on the Indian's back and digging his fingers into his face. His two older brothers jump into the fray. But the wiry Indian has an unexpected strength. Despite three and a weakened Lewis wrestling him, he manages to get off a shot.

The Sheikh is slow to realise what is happening until the zing of a passing bullet clears his head.

On the other side of the curtain, the captain jumps up on hearing the commotion and draws his revolver. His mind is yet to clear of drowsiness. Noises are coming from two opposite directions. He spins his head and gun around to where the kitchen is, back to the men's quarters and back to the kitchen again. The decision of which fracas to sort out first is made by his corporal. He crashes through the curtain with three men and a boy hanging off him.

More yelling from the other direction and the captain has had enough. He points his pistol in the air and fires off a shot. The three brothers freeze and the corporal frees himself from the tangle of arms and legs. He takes control of his rifle and stands with his captain. A dazed and nauseous Lewis is on hands and knees trying to shake the recent storm out of his head.

A single gunshot had little effect in halting the ruckus coming from the kitchen. The captain orders his corporal to take guard once again over the men while he goes to investigate.

What he sees is of no great concern to him.

After ridding himself of burning embers, Private Mashinter's built-up rage is desperately in need of releasing on someone. Stopped from taking advantage of A'isha has left him also frustrated.

Faizah sits defiantly upright puffing on her pipe. Her tattooed face shines with a smearing of palm oil. Her moist eyes stare unblinking into the onlooking captain's. From behind, a crazed Gilbert Mashinter starts to molest her.

On the other side of the open fireplace with its scattered embers and cooking plate, Sergeant Claverdon has A'isha cornered. Her hands are tightly held behind her back and she's turned a little to one side to avoid another attempted kick to his groin. His free hand is around A'isha's neck as he starts to lick and kiss her. Her struggles are useless under his strength and weight.

The captain turns his eyes away from the old woman's stare, surveys the kitchen scene before him then allows a broad smile to liven up his broad moustache. His men have earned such a reward for their misdeeds and loyalty. Now is the time for him to turn up the heat. He returns to join his Indian corporal standing guard over the males. With his raised pistol, he directs all to join their women in the food preparation area.

The scene that awaits the Sheikh and his sons angers and sickens them. Qamrani goes to run to his mother but a hand on his collar pulls him back. The older sons make a move to stop her violation. The cocking of a pistol pressed against their young brother's head brings them to a halt. The Sheikh makes his attempt to rescue his wife. The corporal's rifle butt to the head knocks him to the ground where he lies unconscious. Jumaa and Runmaiz attempt to go to his aid, but guns pointing at them and Qamrani has them defenceless, controlled and tortured witnesses to the assault on their mother and a young Bedouin girl.

Faizah turns her face to her sons with a plea for them to resist any attempt at stopping what is to happen. It will only end in their death, and that is not what she believes Allah has in mind for them.

Lewis has yet to regain his energy and shake off the cloudiness in his head. But the sight before him brings back images of the abuse some of the white cattlemen forced on Aboriginal women. His rage aids the restoration of some energy. He goes to make a move but the captain is quicker and aims his revolver between Lewis' eyes.

A'isha's mind is also focussing on the past. Not distant, but recent! The scrambled memory of how she became injured begins to unravel. Still unclear in a visual sense, but the closeness of the sergeant has hit on her sense of smell.

She has turned to face her frenzied and aroused abuser. His hand has left her face and is undoing the top button of his shirt. A'isha tries to divert her eyes from looking at the man's sweating flesh. But something has grabbed her attention. The unbuttoned shirt has revealed a talisman hanging around the sergeant's neck. It's not the same as her own, but they are exactly the three parcels she tried to replicate…they're her mother's.

Her mind begins to clear. It was not the Australians who raided her camp, but these men. And it was this man, this bastard of a sergeant, who attacked her mother. She had tried to stop the brutality, but an arm wrenched and twisted behind her and a hit to the head is all she recalls. But the odour of the man who did it left its mark. She now accepts that it was the Australians who happened across the assault and rescued her.

With the image now clear in her mind, she aims her stare into the frenzied eyes of her attacker. Like a magnet, he's forced to stare back. The veins in his eyes start to bleed. His grip on her hands relaxes enough for her to grasp her talisman with one hand and her mother's with the other.

A deathly silence spreads throughout the tent and surrounding desert.

Outside, the camels stop chewing and turn their heads towards the kitchen area. The gang's horses pound the ground with their hooves and pull on their reins looped around one of the tent posts. Spade's eyes are wide and white. His head is rocking from side. He sniffs at the developing willy-willy swirling around him. Then watches as it spins its way into the tent.

Veils and tunics start flapping in the wind. The Indian corporal's turban unravels, allowing his long hair to whip into his face and eyes. In a blind moment, he grabs at the horseshoe around his neck. The union of horseshoe and nail rings on his fingers create a hollow sound that douses the wind. A'isha is flung backwards into one of the tent posts. Her grasp on the sergeant's amulet breaks the twine tied around his neck and for a moment all appear frozen in a bubble of time.

To A'isha, it's like staring into a still photograph. She sees the family of Bedouin and the boy soldier under guarded control. The Sheikh lies unconscious on the ground. The private is kneeling behind the old woman with his hands around her body. And the sergeant looks ready to launch himself at her again. But the Indian is the one she fears most. He's looking back at her with a smug, arrogant look of a man who has the ability and power to exorcise spirits.

I'm confused. The talismans in my hands do not hold spirits but help protect me from them. Then why, Allah, why have I been thrust aside by this man's power?

She feels a tremor run through the length of her body. All her nerves being to tingle and her eyes close, yet she continues to see all around her.

Is this the truth I was never meant to see? Is this my destiny never intended to be discovered? Is this the reason I have no voice?

With eyes still closed, she rises to her feet. Lifted rather than of her own doing. She straightens up with outstretched arms. In one hand she holds her talisman and in the other her mother's.

Oh, it is now so clear to me. It lay hidden until this very moment. I have no voice because, at birth, it was replaced by the spirit of a Djinn.

In a surprise move to all, including herself, she claps her hands together. The sound it creates is louder and sharper than the crack of lightening. The two talismans become one in a burst of energy that sends all but A'isha lurching back as if by a strong gust of wind…yet the carpet walls of the tent remain still.

The Indian appears unaffected and goes to again grab at his horseshoe.

A'isha has come to the crossroads in her life. To continue to be as she has all her life or to accept what she has always had the ability to be…a Djinn! And the time is now!

The Indian has used his powers to repel me once and most likely will again if I do not have help.

There is only one other she can turn to. The one she has sensed has his own powers. She opens her eyes, and, as if waiting for her, Lewis is staring back.

He is still in need of energy, but I see a depth of reserve. I pray his ancestral spirits have followed him from his far-away home.

A connection between A'isha and Lewis releases an unearthly chant from the Indian. He grasps the horseshoe around his neck. The air vibrates in the tent. All things metal begin flying around and gathering into a magnetised swirling mass.

Lewis straightens up, only to see A'isha facing the approaching swirling, slicing mass. Her silent cries for help get a response from deep within. He begins the murmuring to his spirits. This distracts the Indian for an instant. Enough time to allow the forging of Lewis' Dreamtime spirits with A'isha's Djinn spirit. The combined forces rattle the Indian. He too needs help from another place and chews on his Khat for a drug-induced hit. His surge of crazed energy lulls the air. All the powers building within the tent ready themselves for battle.

The swirling mass collapses to a metallic heap on the ground. For a moment the Indian, A'isha and Lewis appear in a suspended trance. Not so the captain, sergeant and private, for they are well aware of the Indian's unique talents. It's the girl's and this disguised Australian Aboriginal soldier's talents they are uncertain of. In a flash, they make a grab for the three brothers and Faizah to hold and kill if threatened.

Their sudden movement stirs the merged force created by Lewis and A'isha. Lewis increases the volume of his murmuring while the Indian breathes more power into his chanting. The air in the tent begins to vibrate as if in battle with itself. Then a voice, the likes of which have never been heard before, erupts from the open mouth of A'isha.

The embers in the fire pit begin to glow brighter until they burst into flame. Higher and higher they flare in a dance of creation. Images appear in the raging blaze. Animals, birds, fish, reptiles join as one in a fiery display of living things.

But the Indian has seen the same thing once before. He slaps the horseshoe around his neck with both nail ringed hands. Sparks shower the flames in the pit.

Lewis watches the last flash of brightness as the fire dies down. Weakened, he is ready to accept the Indian has the greater power. The Indian has won.

Lewis looks to A'isha, his eyes offering an apology that his spirits were no match. But A'isha has not moved. Her mouth is still wide open. There is no sound coming from her, only a soft hum of breath seen as a green mist the colour of her scarab still clenched in her hand.

There is movement as the renegade gang ready themselves to do what they always intended to do. Rifles, a pistol and a knife pick their targets.

An agonising groan from the dead fire attracts everyone's attention. The flames have died, but the plumes of smoke left in their place rise higher and higher. Twisting and entwined into themselves the higher they reach. To a choreographed dance, images form. Not birds, fish, animals or reptiles, but human faces. As the smoke rises to the height of the tent, a combined image takes shape. A human form made up of crying, screaming, tortured faces. The captain, sergeant and private recognise their voices coming from the smoky figure. Each study all the faces until seeing themselves. As soon as they make eye contact with their own image, the same agonising screams bellow from their mouths. They drop their weapons to cover their ears, but the sounds are coming from within and cannot be silenced. In a frenzied panic they succumb and collapse in a squirming heap.

Runmaiz, Jumaa and Qamrani start gathering together all the dropped weapons. But the Indian continues to fight off this attack. In a last-ditched effort, he slaps his hands onto his horseshoe with greater force. Mixed with the shower of sparks is his high-pitched wail. A word becomes recognisable…a name he has conjured up from his inner powers…a name no one else was aware of…A'isha!

Her mouth closes, her eyes go blank, and she sinks to the ground. Her grip on both talismans relaxes, allowing them to roll away from her.

With the girl overpowered, it leaves only the soldier for the Indian corporal to deal with. He turns to Lewis to scan his mind for a name that will render him useless.

Lewis accepts that his chances of saving Spade are over, and, possibly for the last time, silently murmurs his name.

The Indian smiles as he relishes another victory over the spirits of the desert and calls out the name. But it's not the one he had conjured up. It's not Lewis…but SPADE!

To his surprise, the rear wall of the tent is violently torn down by Spade. In a frenzy, the Indian turns to another chant. He's about to slam his hands onto his horseshoe again but Spade beats him. He rears up to full height and slams his injured hoof into the horseshoe around the Indian's neck. The clash of the two horseshoes reverses the power of the Indian and sends his body into spasms. No human can endure such internal force. His body becomes a magnet pressing all the iron he wears into his skin. The nail rings tighten, severing his fingers so they drop one by one to the ground. The horseshoe around his neck transforms into a deep reddish scar that will forever be a permanent reminder. He collapses.

Chapter 24
FREEDOM

[A'isha]

It's amazing how so much devastation can be confined to such a small area while the rest of the tent and surrounds remain undisturbed. The real war may be over, but the war between forces of a different kind has left its mark.

In stark contrast to the wreckage of the kitchen's workings, the calmness that now prevails in the air offers peace long forgotten.

Working around the obstruction of a horse in the confined space, Qamrani is helping his mother clear up the mess and get the kitchen back to how she likes it. The captain, sergeant and private are securely shackled and still to come to terms with what has happened. The corporal lies an unconscious, twisted wreck. Crude bandages cover the stumps of both hands, but internal injuries will render him disabled for the rest of his miserable life. The Sheikh is resting his throbbing head. Jumaa and Runmaiz have gone to retrieve the gang's spooked horses and a couple of the camels that ran off.

A'isha remains slumped on her knees. Her energy is wasted. Both talismans lay on the ground before her. She reaches out, retrieves them, kissing them both before holding them tight to her chest.

In front of her, the boy soldier has his arms around his horse's neck. Partly to support his weakened body, but more importantly to celebrate the beginning of a new life together.

The union of our spirits has done its work. The desert will now give us our freedom.

[Lewis]

The feel of his horse's head nestled into his neck is hard to break. There is a closeness never felt before, bound by the realisation their ancestral spirits have followed them all this way to their new land. Compared to what they have been through, nothing can get in the way of their freedom now.

With the sun beginning to set, the time to test that freedom is now. The three days of the Sheikh's protection are over, yet in the end, it was Lewis who became the protector. No one will stop them from leaving now, not even Runmaiz

Lewis leads Spade to the second water bag that has been waiting for him. While Spade drinks, Lewis begins to sort through the scattered mess. With the help of a saddened but understanding Qamrani, they gather together whatever food is recoverable. The water bag is refilled and tied at the neck with a strip of leather. It's then fastened to the parcel of food and hung over Spade's neck. Lewis has a last check on the injured hoof. Any sign of inflammation or bruising has disappeared. The coming together with the corporal's horseshoe has healed all damage, including the cuts to his rump. Satisfied Spade is fit enough to carry his weight; he mounts his horse for the first time since arriving at the army camp on their way to Kantara.

He looks back to the family that has now gathered before him. The gang is secure and under the control of Jumaa and Runmaiz. Bedouin law will determine their fate. Qamrani has fastened his eyes on Lewis with tears running down his cheeks. Lewis nods to him, knowing the spirit that lives alongside the boy will protect him and his family and ensure he will be the one to succeed his father.

[A'isha]

A'isha also has tears in her eyes as she waits to see her boy soldier and his horse ride out of her life. She falsely accused him of her pain and now regrets she has been a thorn in his side since stealing his horse.

If only I could speak, I would offer you my heartfelt apology. I have wronged you and that will be enough for you to refuse my forgiveness. I will miss you my boy soldier.

Lewis has steered Spade to her side. Their eyes meet. Will this be the last time? A'isha raises her hand holding her mother's talisman and offers it to him.

Go my boy soldier with my mother's protection. May it remind you of this silly Bedouin girl you once knew.

Lewis reaches down to take the talisman. Their hands meet. For a moment, A'isha's wish of being pulled aboard Spade may come true. But it's shattered as Lewis accepts the talisman and their hands part. She bows her head and closes her eyes to imprint in her mind this final image of horse and rider. She hears the shifting of his seat on Spade as he prepares to ride off. Then feels a soft touch under her chin. She raises her head. His hand outstretched. She looks up and sees the smile on his face and her mother's talisman hanging around his neck. She looks back down to his offered hand, back up to his beaming face then to the Bedouin family watching on. The Sheikh and Qamrani are also smiling. Without hesitation, she grabs hold of Lewis' hand and allows herself to be lifted onto Spades' back. Spade gives a shake of his head and a look back to make sure his new passenger is well seated. His master's gentle nudge from sandalled feet is the beginning of their journey together.

Chapter 25
EL ARISH

[A'isha and Lewis]

The breeze from the Mediterranean Sea ruffles the tent stalls filling the El Arish marketplace. Families are enjoying the return of peace to their region. Children run around playing without fear or restriction. Their parents and other adults stroll along smiling at all who pass. Some stop to talk; not about the past, but of the future. The babble of bartering is loud and friendly from stalls overflowing with food and items that once again are plentiful.

One small stall is set back off the main plaza that flows to the coast. Its offering is meagre. A small range of Bedouin talismans and some brightly coloured woven fabric. Behind the display sits A'isha. A dish of cloves and a camel skin pouch of alum are beside her. In her hand is a small lump of green soapstone. She is hand carving her third scarab for the day. When finished and polished, she'll hold each scarab firmly in her hand to cast her Djinn spell upon it. They will now carry her spiritual force to help protect the wearer on their desert journeys.

The laughter and cheers of children in the open forum brings a smile to her face. She's heard it so often and yet still can't resist looking. Her boy soldier—now her fellow nomad—is performing tricks on his horse to the delight of all. His bare head radiates with the red of his hair. A clownish touch replicated in the red ochre applied to Spade's mane.

She misses her family, whether they be still on this Earth or not. But she knows her mother looks over them both by the talisman around Lewis' neck.

Yes, she is a Djinn, and so too is Lewis, though in his own, unique cultural and spiritual way. And like A'isha, he too misses his family. But he has found their comfort in his spiritual songline that has followed him to this distant land.

But above of all this, what satisfies him the utmost…he saved Spade.